Published by Amanda McIntyre

WORTH THE WAIT
Copyright © 2018 by Amanda McIntyre

www.amandamcintyresbooks.com

All rights reserved. Except for use in any review, the reproduction or utilization of this work in whole or in part in any form by any electronic, mechanical or other means, now known or hereinafter invented, including xerography, photocopying and recording, or in any information storage or retrieval system, is forbidden without the written permission of the publisher.

This is a work of fiction. Names, characters, places and incidents are either the product of the author's imagination or are used fictitiously, and any resemblance to actual persons, living or dead, business establishments, events or locales is entirely coincidental.

Printed in the USA.

Interior format by

LAST HOPE RANCH

AMANDA MCINTYRE

*To those who believe in second chances
and that love will always find a way*

CHAPTER ONE

"TOO SOON?" BY THE LOOK on Julie's startled face, Hank Richardson figured he'd damn well jumped the gun. In his defense, in the last year and a half since Julie and her two boys had come to live at the Last Hope Ranch, he'd thought things had progressed to the point where the idea seemed approachable.

Apparently, not as much as he'd hoped.

He felt bad. There was nowhere—short of a using a parachute—that the poor woman could go. He'd taken her up in his plane, of all things, thinking that a pass over the beautiful Crazy Mountains against a stunning late-summer sunset would be the perfect setting to pop the question.

So much for *perfect*.

Hank withdrew the small velvet box that held the Tiffany diamond inside, his vision of a romantic marriage proposal disappearing as quickly as the orange sun on the horizon.

"No. I—I'm sorry," she stammered, holding her hand to her heart. She looked like she might be ill. "I just…it's so sudden—"

"Say no more," he said, pocketing the ring in his denim shirt pocket.

She reached over and touched his forearm.

"Hank, I'm flattered—speechless, in fact. It's just…"

"I'm moving too fast, right?" God, he'd have married her a week after her divorce from that psychotic excuse of a husband. Instead, he'd put on the brakes, deciding it was worth the wait. Then again, maybe his sister, Caroline, had been right when she'd accused him of having 'white knight' syndrome.

"Hank," Julie said softly. "You know how much I care about you. You've been so good to me and the boys since we moved here."

He raised his brow. That much was true. He'd flown her brother, Clay Saunders, to California and had wound up taking a bullet in the shoulder during the daring rescue wherein her husband had been holding her and their sons hostage in a domestic dispute.

"You made all the arrangements for us to move here—you and Clay." She sighed. "And I'm forever grateful."

Grateful? Oh hell, he'd *really* gotten it wrong. He tossed her a quick glance, not wanting to let her see his disappointment. Hank had secretly fallen in love with her the first time they'd met in college. She'd come to watch her brother, Clay, play in a football game. The only one of the four friends not involved in that game, Hank had been her designated bodyguard. Lord, he'd fallen hard and fast. But before he could blink twice, she'd gone and gotten engaged, eventually marrying the hot-shot corporate slime ball that moved her as far from her friends and family as he could.

In all the years after she'd never been far from his

thoughts, or his heart. "There's no need to keep a tally, Julie. I've been more than happy to help out. I just thought…well, that things were moving along to the point where it was time to take this… us…to the next level." Even now, her brother, his wife Sally, their family and her two boys along with the friends and families of the Kinnison clan waited back at the ranch in anticipation of a celebratory dinner to mark this engagement.

The hum of the engine seemed to fill the silence, exacerbating the epic fail of his carefully planned evening.

"Hank," she said quietly. "My divorce has only been final for a few months."

It sounded reasonable. His heart felt otherwise. To him it'd been an eternity getting to this moment. The private airstrip came into view. This past year, Hank had spent so much time traveling back and forth between Chicago and End of the Line to see Julie and the boys that the Kinnison brothers had gone ahead and gotten a permit to build the private airstrip, primarily for his use. Even they'd been confident that the relationship had been progressing. "I guess I got a little exuberant."

"Hank—"

He closed his eyes against the gentle tone in her voice that could quicken his heartbeat, dredging up memories of a couple of times when they'd snuck away for quiet dinners, or the surprise trip to New Orleans where'd they'd spent an entire rainy weekend holed up in the Hotel Monteleone. "Listen, you don't owe me any explanations." He reached over and patted her hand. That said, he didn't relish the back-pedaling account he'd have to give to the room of waiting dinner guests.

"You need to let me explain." She shifted in her seat, holding his hand in her lap. "I do see us getting married…eventually. I'm not shopping around. I'm only just beginning to get my feet on the ground. Finding myself again. You can understand that, can't you?"

Hank slid his hand from her grip. "Oh, sure. Yeah," he said with a shrug. He flipped a few switches, focused on the runway, and brought the plane down in a smooth landing on the short strip. He taxied the plane into the hangar and shut off the engine. Staring out the window, he waited a heartbeat, unsure where to go from here. Hank heard her unbuckle.

"Hey, you're not mad, are you? You do understand?" She leaned over and turned his face to meet her gaze. Her hand drifted over his thigh. "Did I mention I believe in long engagements?" she whispered close to his ear. "Maybe I could see the ring again?"

He let his heart hope that he wasn't going to lose her a second time.

"Why don't you unbuckle that belt?" She waited as he did and then crawled into his lap, smiling as she fished in his pocket for the velvet box. She handed it to him. "Ask me again."

"Julie, I—"

She cupped his face, kissing him softly. "Ask me, Hank."

"Fine." He nodded. "Julie, will you marry me?" His heart squeezed at having to ask again.

She held out her hand as he slipped on the sparkling stone. Her eyes welled.

"Those *are* happy tears, right?" He tipped his head, eyeing her.

"Of course. It's beautiful." She kissed him with the same thoroughness that had made him think he'd been on the right road with this idea.

Had Aimee not gone to the trouble of creating the surprise engagement dinner, he might have taken her to his cabin and made this a private party. But the Kinnisons were like brothers and Clay Saunders, Julie's real brother, as much a sibling to him. They were family and he wanted Julie to feel part of that family. He framed her face, kissing her softly, then held her gaze. "I should tell you that there is an engagement party waiting for us back at the ranch." He gave her a rueful smile. "Julie, I love you. I want to spend the rest of my life with you and the boys." He searched her eyes, waiting for her response.

She offered him a tentative smile, then slid back into her seat. "We'd better get going then. Everyone will be waiting."

And just like that her guard was up again. "Jules?" he questioned, about to press her for a response to his declaration of love. Despite the many ways she'd expressed her feelings towards him, she'd yet to say those three little words that would solidify their relationship.

"Yes?" she asked as she fished through her purse and pulled out her lip gloss. The ring on her finger winked in the setting sunlight.

Not wanting to pressure her further, he waved off his concern. "Never mind." He hopped from the cabin and ducked under the wing. Truth was, he should be ecstatic. She'd accepted the ring. They had amazing chemistry. And hadn't she admitted to him that she wanted to get married…albeit eventually? The least he could do is be patient and understand she needed a little time to adjust to her new life. Still, it didn't make it any easier to wait for her to say "I love you."

Taking Julie's hand, Hank smiled as he twirled her into his arms and kissed her softly. "Let's go share our good news, what do you say?"

They'd been at the dinner table less than forty-five minutes. Julie wanted to crawl under the table at the rapid-fire questions assaulting her about their wedding plans.

"Have you set a date?" Aimee asked, her enthusiastic smile an indicator that she'd been thinking about this much longer than Julie had been.

Julie darted Hank a look, silently pleading for his help. Though they hadn't really had time to discuss the reasons in detail, she hoped that, when it came down to it, he'd magically understand why she couldn't yet commit to a date.

"We haven't actually discussed—" Hank began.

"What we want exactly," Julie finished with a smile. The discussion was awkward at best and Aimee seemed oblivious to the tension between Julie and Hank.

"Well, of course," Aimee said. "I'm sure you're still working out the logistics of whether to live in Chicago or here."

Kyle, Julie's oldest, shot a look at his mom. "Mom?" Her pre-teen son's voice cracked as he looked at her with panic in his eyes.

Hank intercepted his concern, lifting his hands. "Whoa, nobody is moving *anywhere*, buddy." He looked from one boy to the other. "When and if that becomes a possibility, we will all decide it together, okay?"

"Oh, goodness, absolutely," Aimee said, realizing her *faux pas*. "I guess what I meant to say was when you get to the point of planning, Wyatt and I want you to know that the ranch is at your disposal. There's plenty of room for guests in the cabins and with a little work, the barn is a beautiful place for a reception."

Wyatt reached over, took Aimee's hand, and pressed a kiss to her knuckles. "Aimee's right." Wyatt's quick glance at Hank wasn't lost on Julie. "Whenever you two are ready. You know that you can just ask, and we'll all be there for you. Anything you need, okay?"

Julie wanted to ask everyone to take a step back and allow them time to breathe. It wasn't as though she hadn't thought this day—Hank proposing marriage—would happen, but there'd been no hint in recent weeks that he was about to pop the all-important question. "Thank you. All of you," Julie said, then offered a nervous laugh. "My goodness. When I think about everything that's going on, I can't see where we'd possibly add a wedding." She looked at each one seated around the table, hoping her fear to commit wasn't blatantly showing. "Kyle has that big adventure Scout trip in Colorado coming up and, well, all of us are involved in the big Frontier Days celebration." She glanced around at the faces staring at her. "And there's the railroad museum opening, too."

Hank glanced down at his plate.

Julie suddenly felt as though she was the bad guy in all of this. While she'd only been engaged for less than a few hours, it seemed that everyone here had assumed this was an inevitable outcome and that they'd marry quickly.

Liberty, who'd been silent up to now, spoke up. "You know it's pretty amazing, since we've been advertising the celebration and dedication of the depot to the National Registry of Historic places, the cabins are starting to get booked already. Seems like a lot of people are interested in the museum dedication."

Rein nodded. "That's true, and the cook-off Betty wants to do is going to be a big draw to the community as well," he said, helping his son, Cody take a no-thank you helping of peas on his plate.

"We've already started freezing pies at the bakery to get ready for the population explosion," Rebecca Greyfeather offered.

Julie wanted to hug Rein and Liberty for coming to her aid. "Oh," she said holding her hands to her cheeks. "I almost forgot about the cook-off."

"To be fair," Rein continued, "with the website Liberty launched for the Last Hope Ranch, we've already scheduled two corporate retreats for late summer. And we can't forget the annual trail ride we offer for free to Miss Ellie and her moms and kids at the shelter."

Hank slipped his hand over Julie's, which was fisted nervously in her lap. "Thanks, all of you," he said. "It's nice to know we have the ranch as an option and, more importantly, your support and blessings." He picked up his water glass and held it aloft. "To family."

"Here, here," Dalton said with a grin and lifted his water glass. "And, on that note, I'm afraid I need to get this little guy home." He tipped his head toward the high chair where little Sawyer Kinnison had fallen asleep.

Julie looked at the slumbering child, remembering her own at that age. Would she and Hank have children? It was more than clear that family was important to him. Julie's eyes were drawn to the child's head resting on the tray, his little mouth curled in an adorable pout. Dark brown ringlets, much the same as Dalton's, covered his head.

Dalton carefully removed the bib from around the boy's neck. "His mama and sister should be back by now from Billings. Angelique thought she and Emilee needed some mother-daughter time after her doctor's appointment today."

Rebecca appeared from the kitchen holding a covered pie. She tucked it inside the diaper bag Dalton had slung over his shoulder. "Thanks, Rebecca. I may save some for the girls." He tossed her an ornery grin.

"Tell Angelique we missed her and Emilee," Liberty said. "And tell her I'll stop by tomorrow to see if she needs anything."

Dalton plopped his ballcap on his son's head. "Tea and crackers if you stop by in the morning. I'm glad that school is out and Em can be around some to help more during the day." A flash of concern shimmered in his dark eyes. "She said she can't remember feeling this badly with either Em or Sawyer."

Clay glanced at Sally, and they shared a smile before he spoke. "It'll be interesting to hear what Doc says." Clay had a wicked grin on his face as he spoke. "Maybe the twin stork has blessed you guys, as well."

Dalton shot Clay a shocked look.

Rebecca patted Dalton's shoulder. "A little pie and a cup of tea might settle her stomach. Be sure it's chamomile."

Dalton nodded and, followed by a chorus of farewells, left with his son.

Rebecca turned to the rest of the table and took orders for some of her famous peach pie.

"If you'll excuse me," Aimee said. "I'm going to go check on Ezekiel. He fell asleep while we were fixing supper. I want to make sure he's not coming down with something."

"I can do that, sweetheart," Wyatt offered halfway out of his chair.

She kissed his cheek. "I'll be right back." Placing her hand on her protruding belly she waddled down the hall to the nursery.

"How are the riding lessons coming?" Hank asked Chris and Kyle. Since their move to End of the Line, Michael Greyfeather and Clay's wife, Sally, had taken it upon themselves to teach the boys to ride. Hank had been meaning to take them for a trail ride as soon as he finished up this last round of client trips.

"They're naturals." Sally smiled. "As good as any students I've had."

Julie noted that her boys beamed at the compliment.

"Course, if they're serious about the junior roping contest during the rodeo, they're going to have to practice more with Michael." Sally crooked a brow and pinned them with a grin.

Julie shot her sister-in-law an inquisitive look. "Excuse me, what rodeo? What roping contest?"

"Mom," Kyle said, his eyes alive with excitement. "Coach Reed is setting up a rodeo out at his place for Frontier Days. He's offering a junior roping contest and the winner gets one hundred bucks and a trophy!"

Julie made a mental note to speak with Justin about adding a junior competition. She looked at Hank, unsure where her boys felt they had the permission to participate in the event. "I'm not sure that's such a good idea. You're just learning to ride a horse. We probably need to talk more about this."

"Jules," Clay said, stepping in to defend his nephew. "Both the boys are doing very well on a horse. And"—he pointed at Michael, then Wyatt—"I understand that those two are the best ropers in the state."

Aha! Clay, the encourager. Julie narrowed her gaze on him.

Wyatt held up his palm. "I doubt that—"

Rein stopped him. "You can't deny it, big brother. I can remember Jed grooming you on cattle drives."

"Yeah, well, I haven't done any ropin' in quite some time." Wyatt threw a dubious look at Rein. He and Dalton had been in their teens when a car accident had taken the lives of Rein's folks and

Jed's only sister. By then, Jed had adopted both Wyatt and Dalton as his own, just before their mom abandoned them and ran off with a Las Vegas tycoon. With Jed as their guide, the four men became as close as any blood family.

Michael grinned. "I can remember how good you were, Wyatt. It'd help Kyle a lot to learn your technique."

The debate continued, being batted back and forth with exaggerated stories, jabs at one another ending in laughter, and eventually agreeing to disagree, until another opinion ignited the whole thing again.

It wasn't that they argued, Julie thought as she ate her pie and observed the discussion. It's how they approached life—fearless, open, offering praise for each other as much as suggestions for improvement.

She glanced at her sons, totally immersed in the display of friendly male conversation, done amiably without malice, without anger. Yielding, offering thoughts—the way people should handle resolutions.

Hank hammered back, tossing out stories from the past, every now and again pointing to the boys and cautioning them not to do what they did as reckless youths. Julie smiled at how he included them in the conversation.

"I think sometimes they just enjoy getting each other riled up," Sally whispered to Julie, leaning toward her conspiratorially.

She saw her brother laughing out loud, enjoying being around his friends—she hadn't seen that until she lived here and saw him surrounded by

WORTH THE WAIT

the love and support of the men seated at this table.

Wyatt slapped his palm to the table, garnering everyone's attention. He smiled at Kyle, who then straightened, sitting a bit taller in his chair. "Okay, okay. I'll gladly show you boys a thing or two. But on one condition only." He pointed his finger at Kyle, his gaze bouncing to Julie and back to Kyle. "Only if your mom says its okay," Wyatt said. "Number one rule in this house is when mama's not happy, nobody's happy." Wyatt smiled at Aimee as she returned to her seat. "Isn't that so, darlin'? How's Ezekiel?"

"He's sleeping soundly. But I turned on the cool mist vaporizer, as a precaution," she said. "As to the house rule. I've taught you well, darlin." Aimee patted his shoulder "Rebecca, this peach pie looks totally sinful. I'm probably going to need another piece." Aimee smiled at Liberty as she patted her tummy.

Kyle touched his mother's arm. "Mom, please, may I learn how to rope?" he asked.

CHAPTER TWO

Hank watched as Julie debated how to respond. Her oldest son, who rarely showed interest in anything but video games, held her gaze, seeking her approval.

Her brother, Clay, tossed her a cautionary glance. His relationship with his nephews since their arrival was a natural extension of the long-distance connection he'd maintained with them through video games.

"Fine," she said. "But promise me you'll be careful." She cast a pointed look at her brother. "And I'm holding you responsible if anything happens to him."

Clay winked and raised his hand to offer a high five to his young nephew. "Mamas don't let your babies grow up to be cowboys," he sang off-key.

A round of catcalls followed. Hank smiled, enjoying watching Julie interact with the family he'd come to know almost better than his own. They were salt-of-the-earth folk and he knew Julie had nothing to worry about with either of her sons in the care of Michael and Wyatt.

Hank turned to his long-time friend. "Clay, Dalton mentioned the other day something about you being chosen as marshal for the Frontier Days

WORTH THE WAIT

parade. Congrats, man, that's quite the honor."

Sally beamed proudly at her husband. "They are planning to honor all the veterans in End of the Line and the surrounding towns," she said. "We're hoping to coincide it with the train depot opening since a great many vets returned via the train after World War II. I think it was a bus terminal during the sixties."

"And we have veterans living still in the assisted living home. We're planning on finding a way to transport them on a flat bed, if we can find a way to secure a few wheelchairs," Rein offered.

"You know, come to think of it, I think Nan over at the sporting goods store may still have a short flatbed out on the farm. Her husband used it to haul hay bales back when the farm was operational," Wyatt said. "I can check into if you'd like me to."

Rein nodded. "That's a great idea. And Mr. Saunders over there can lead the parade around the square. You been practicing your princess wave, man?" he asked with a grin.

Clay shot Rein a look as much as to say what he could do with his remark.

"Hey, Jules, how are the plans coming along? Sally mentioned you're getting your committee together."

Julie finished a bite of her pie, and washed it down with a sip of wine. She smiled, looking as though she was happy to have a topic she was more comfortable in discussing. She dived right in, her enthusiasm evident. "Emilee actually came up with the idea of a frontier-days cook-off. We were thinking of maybe having a contest for campfire recipes."

"That sounds like fun." Aimee leaned back, shifting her body, it seemed, to accommodate the growing baby inside her. This wasn't her child, but she loved it as though it was her own. She and Wyatt had been blessed with a healthy baby boy last summer. They'd named him Ezekiel after Jed's great-great grandfather Christian Ezekiel Kinnison, who had once served in the Union Army during the War Between the States. After a brief time in Colorado, he and his family had moved to Montana, and the rest, as Wyatt likes to say, is the Kinnison legacy.

Rein and Liberty had had a number of unsuccessful attempts at getting pregnant before agreeing to become foster parents, and they eventually added Cody to their family through adoption. Soon after, Liberty got pregnant, but miscarried early. Tests run showed that she was not able to carry to term. It was Aimee and Wyatt who stepped forward to suggest they find a surrogate to carry the child. And it was then that Aimee offered to carry their child herself. They began the process right away, and Aimee announced she was pregnant just after the first of the new year, due in late November.

Even after all these years, Hank still marveled at how the close-knit family steadfastly supported one another. He was similarly impressed by how warmly Julie and her boys had been welcomed both at the ranch and by the community. They'd been given a cabin to live in and Betty had offered her a good job with benefits. Still, Hank imagined that their kindness was a bit overwhelming, given the years Julie had spent living under the thumb of an abusive and controlling husband.

"Jerry will be all over this cook-off," Michael said. "I remember when he and Betty used to travel down to Texas for cook-off contests when they were just starting up the diner. He won a lot of contests in his day."

"That's what I understand," Julie interjected. "We were thinking maybe he'd head up the judging for the event."

Michael nodded. "That sounds like a fine idea."

Julie smiled. "In fact, we've had quite a time pinning down impartial judges in this town with so many of us involved in the diner and the bakery. But I think I'm going to suggest Reverend Cook and maybe Nathan from the drugstore. Nan has agreed to take over our veteran's float with Clay as Grand Marshall." Julie nodded toward her brother.

"Oh, which reminds me." Sally looked at Julie. "Don't we have a meeting coming up?"

Julie had to stop and think. "I think we decided Tuesday afternoon at the diner."

Tuesday. Hank mentally slapped himself. He'd forgotten that he had to meet a client in Chicago in the morning—a wealthy, retired corporate president from Chicago and some of his friends who were going to a posh Arizona resort for their annual golf trip.

He'd only be gone a few days, but given the awkward proposal, perhaps it was a good time to step back and give Julie some room to think.

Sally nodded. "I've got to write that down in my planner," she said. "As soon as I can find it."

She laughed.

"Check the toybox," Clay suggested.

A squawk from one of Clay's and Sally's eighteen-month-old twins imprisoned in the playpen demanded attention.

Hank watched awestruck as one of the girls struggled to remove her sister's sock, much to the twin's dismay. Persistent squeals turned into a loud a howl as the affronted sister brought a toy horse down promptly on her sister's head.

"They really do love each other." Sally stood and glanced at Clay. "Time to get the girls home. We refer to bedtime as the witching hour," she said with a wry grin. "Around our house, that can tend to be an organizational challenge."

"Nightmare is the word you're looking for, honey." Clay chuckled, leaned over the playpen, and picked up both girls, holding them like tiny human footballs under each arm.

Hank sat a moment observing his friend, and thinking how all of their lives had changed. Clay, switching out plans for a potential football career to become a Ranger in the Army. His sacrifice to his country had taken its toll, until he'd come to the ranch at Dalton's and Hank's insistence and had met Sally. Then there was Dalton. Good lord, he'd never thought he'd see the day Dalton Kinnison became a father. Of the four of them who had run around at college together, Dalton was the least likely candidate for fatherhood. But fate had intervened, bringing his first love, Angelique, back to town in the wake of a dangerous relationship. Not long after, he'd discovered that Emilee, who'd been raised by Michael and Rebecca Greyfeather, was his daughter from one night spent with Angelique back in high school. This revelation was followed by a tumultuous courtship, but eventually love found a way and the two were given a second chance. Now married, their family was thriving with Emilee and Sawyer and another on the way.

Rein, the one dubbed 'practical with a business head,' had found love with Liberty, the unexpected surprise of a step-sister to Dalton and Wyatt from their estranged mother. The two had faced much together, nearly losing each other in the process, but love had prevailed once more with the solidarity and support of the Kinnison clan.

They'd all faced obstacles, been through the mill and come out with their happily ever afters, as it were. Hank could only hope that he and Julie would be as fortunate.

Julie smiled as she gazed at her brother—he'd been through so much. Once a potential pro football player, his deployments as an Army Ranger had squashed that idea when an IED (Improvised Explosive device) took part of his leg, leaving him scarred both physically and emotionally. But accepting Hank's invitation to visit the Last Hope Ranch had started him down a path of healing. And then he'd met Sally, the town's elementary school music teacher, and it had changed her brother in ways she hadn't thought possible.

When little Ava and Aubrey had first come home from the hospital, Julie had still been reeling from her own life drama, but helping with the girls, seeing her boys with their newborn cousins, had been the key in getting past the initial ramifications of the trauma they'd all experienced.

Even now, Julie clung to the security of having Clay and his family nearby. And it had been at his advice that she'd visited with Reverend Leslie Cook, pastor of the First Church of Christ, who'd been instrumental in helping Clay wade though some tough emotions when he arrived at the Last Hope Ranch.

In a flurry of chaos and laughter, everyone helped to gather and pack up what Clay lovingly referred to as their "traveling circus." With the last harness buckled on the car seats and the playpen stored in the truck bed, Clay and Sally made their rounds with hugs and thanks.

Kyle pulled his uncle to his level and whispered in his ear. She saw Clay glance at her and nod.

"Mom, can we stay at Uncle Clay's tonight?" he asked. Impossibly charming with a wide smile, mischievous blue eyes, and surfer blonde hair like her ex, Julie had to practice caution with this one. He knew no fear and had an independent streak a mile wide. Hank joked that one day he'd be a handful around the ladies.

"We could help with Aubrey and Ava," Chris, her youngest, pleaded with soulful brown eyes. He'd been gifted with the Saunders side of the family's dark brown eyes and impossibly long lashes but also his father's tendency toward a hair-trigger temper.

In the past couple of weeks, Julie had convinced Chris to accompany her to see Reverend Cook. Julie had hoped that the pastor's experience working with troubled teens would help where she hadn't been able to as of late. Part of the disconnect between them was the anger toward his father and toward God. Seeing his father threaten them with a gun had left a deep scar of betrayal in Chris's heart. Reverend Cook explained to her that Chris's anger was a defense against emotions he wasn't sure how to deal with, that no kid should ever have to deal with.

"Actually, that'd be great. I could use their help with some stuff I have to do around the house tomorrow, if that's okay. What do you say?" Clay glanced at his nephews. "You guys up for that?"

"Yeah!" they answered in unison.

"We've got stuff for them back at the house from the last sleepover," Sally said, tousling Chris's hair.

Julie hugged each of her sons. "I suppose." She pointed at her brother. "But don't keep them up too late playing video games."

"Come on, Jules," Clay scoffed even as his mouth curled in a wicked grin. "Would I do that?" He pulled her into a bear hug. "Don't worry, Sis. They'll be in bed before midnight."

Everyone filtered out onto the front porch exchanging hugs and appreciation for the lovely evening. Congratulations for their engagement was decidedly more subdued.

Watching the last car drive away, Wyatt placed his arm around his pregnant wife's shoulder. "You need to get off your feet," he said.

"Thank you, Aimee," Julie said, offering the woman a quick hug. Wyatt shook Hank's hand. Julie overheard his quiet congratulations before Wyatt draped his arm around his wife's shoulder and steered her inside.

The door closed, the lights shut off. Hank and Julie stood alone on the gravel drive. An awkward pause followed. Julie hated the feeling brought on by this recent change in their relationship. She wanted to feel happy, in that giddy, new-love way. And Hank should be happy.

Instead, there seemed to be a divide between them that she was at a loss of how to bridge. True, setting a date, making a commitment to married life seemed the obvious solution. But there was a disconnect between her heart and head. Reverend Cook had tried to encourage her by saying she needed to give herself time to trust again, to believe in romance again after such a severe betrayal.

Julie had gnawed long and hard on that thought. Glad for the sort of relationship she had with Hank, she admitted it was based on physical intimacy more than emotional—but even that had been a big step, in her mind. She wasn't quite ready yet to entrust her whole self—body and soul—to another person.

"Come on, let's walk." He slipped his hand in hers and led her over to the corral where a few of the horses were grazing. The sky was clear, awash with a million stars, and the scent of sweet grass blew with the soft summer night breeze. She loved its clean, calming scent and had been taught by Rebecca that it was often used in cleansing rituals, to remove negative energies.

Julie rested her arms over the rail and hoped it would aid in relieving some of the tension she felt she'd caused this evening between herself and

Hank. The brown mare sauntered over to the fence and nuzzled her hand. Its velvety softness made her smile. She heard Hank chuckle.

"Seems she likes you," he said.

Julie glanced at him. This was the man who'd risked life and limb to come to her rescue. He'd been her rock ever since. His feelings for her were clear as the mountain air and his love apparent in many ways. He deserved more than the milquetoast answer she'd given him. And while she wanted to express her emotions, the truth was, she'd been fooled once by what she thought was true love and it had turned out to be disastrous. How could she know this was any more real than what she'd once felt for Louis?

"You okay?" he asked, tucking a strand of hair behind her ear. "You look lost in your thoughts."

She glanced at him. "I suppose I am. Sorry." She turned, stepping onto the asphalt service road that wound down in front of the cabins that made up the guest houses of the Last Hope Ranch. The road, put in for ease of traveling the hilly terrain, wound down past the stables and training paddocks. The cabins were spaced far enough apart to allow for privacy, yet close enough to be connected to all the systems required for comfort.

He caught up to her and took her hand. "Jules, are you having second thoughts about this—about us?"

He stood there, his heart in his hand, waiting for her to respond with something firm, reciprocal to his emotions. How could she explain that she didn't want to change the good thing they already had? "It's not that—"

He tugged her to a stop. "Not *that*?" His dark gaze pierced hers in the light of the street lamps dotting the path. Confusion was etched into his handsome face. She couldn't blame him—she was just as confused by her response. Here was her white knight, ready to whisk her away to a blissful happily ever after. What was wrong with her?

"I don't know how to explain what it is I'm feeling, Hank. I'm, afraid you might not understand." She tried to remember what she'd learned in her therapy sessions, hoping to find the words to adequately explain her reluctance.

"You know what? Maybe this whole thing isn't such a good idea." He edged around her, hands stuffed in his pockets, and started down the road.

She caught up to him and grabbed his arm. "This is exactly what I was afraid would happen."

He paused, eyes fixed on the ground. "You know, Julie, you *can* say no." He shrugged and then and looked up at her. "I don't want you to say yes out of some misguided sense of obligation."

"Hank." She cupped his face and shook her head. "No, that's not it, either."

He turned from her grasp, sighed, and met her gaze. "What are we doing here, Jules? What's happening?"

They stood on the dimly lit path in front of his cabin. As Julie looked at him, time spun backward to the night he'd driven her to the hotel she'd stayed at when visiting her brother at school. She'd suspected even then that he had feelings for her. But disinterested, she'd delicately set them aside, dreaming of bigger and better things—finding a man of substance and social standing, not a man who had lofty dreams and found true richness in a beautiful sunset. But he'd changed. Beyond his broad shoulders and scruffy beard, he'd become comfortable in Wranglers, boots, and a worn bomber jacket he'd picked up in an Army surplus store. The first time she'd seen him walking across the tarmac from his plane, with his confident stride, aviator glasses, and worn ball cap, her heart had done a little flip.

She searched those dark eyes in the shadows, seeing the tick in his firm jaw as he stared at her, waiting for an answer. She dropped her hands to her sides. "My feelings for you haven't changed." She hugged her arms and looked around. "Can we please go inside and talk?"

They walked in silence to her cabin, where Hank unlocked the door and held it open. Standing in the soft glow of the living room light, she tried to remember if she'd left it on accidently. She noticed two flutes and a bucket chilling with a bottle of champagne at the end of the breakfast island—no doubt more of the great lengths to which he'd gone to celebrate their engagement.

Without a word, Hank poured each of them a glass. He leaned against the counter. "Go ahead. I'm listening." He took a long swallow.

Julie sighed softly. "This isn't how I wanted this night to end."

He blew out a sigh and lifted his glass. "Agreed."

Noticing a glow coming from the bedroom, Julie glanced at Hank and walked over to look inside. She clamped her hand over her mouth, tears stinging her eyes as she took in the sight—electric candles flickered on every surface around the room, and rose petals had been strewn across the bedcovers.

"It appears everyone had planned for a different outcome tonight," she murmured, stepping further into the room to take it all in.

She turned to find Hank leaning against the door. He didn't look like a man who'd just gotten engaged, Julie realized, her heart twisting. She wanted to marry him. She did. Just not now. Not as soon as Hank wanted.

"Hank, I want you to understand something."

He raised a brow. "I'm all ears, Julie. Make me understand why, when I tell the woman I love how I feel, tell her that I want to spend the rest of my life with her and be a father to her boys"—he paused—"she can't seem to give me a solid response."

She put down the flute and walked up to him, close enough that she felt the sexual tension crackle between them as it always did. "No man has ever treated me as well as you do, Hank," she said, searching his eyes.

A short laugh escaped his throat. "Not that it's made a difference, apparently."

"I'm not explaining myself very well." She was going to have to kick it up a notch to get her point across. She held his gaze, lifted her summer dress above her hips and drew her panties off one leg at a time. She dangled them from her fingertip.

That seemed to have garnered his attention.

"What I'm trying to say, albeit poorly, is that I have never felt so free to be myself around a man. To feel so beautiful, so sexy…so wanted."

She began to unbutton his shirt and he finished

the job, tearing it off his shoulders and tossing it across the room. Backing her to the bed, he framed her face in a kiss that went on forever, drugging her senses. The backs of her knees grew weak.

"I want more than having fun, Julie." He held her gaze as she grappled for his waistband.

"I know you do," she sighed against his lips.

Julie held his gaze. "I want to marry…someday. But right now, I'm happy with the way we are." She pulled his head down into a fierce kiss knowing where it would lead, perhaps hoping the distraction would be enough to buy her some time to explain, perhaps simply hoping that it would appease his need for a verbal commitment.

He pulled from her, his gaze piercing. "I have loved you from the moment we met back at that damn football game. I'll do whatever you want. Wait as long as you need. I just need to know that you feel for me what I feel for you."

She swallowed the lump in her throat. Her ex had been suave, and what she'd thought was seductive had turned out to be manipulative—part of his need to control her. To make her the wife he thought she should be. "Hank, you understand what I've been through. I know you're nothing like Louis." She searched his eyes. "I'm not even sure I deserve you."

He sighed and leaned his forehead to hers. "You know that's not true."

She waded further into the murky waters of her swirling emotions. "I need a little more time. My head's saying one thing, but my heart's saying another," she said.

His smile was warm. "And you need time for them to catch up and be on the same page."

She nodded. "My heart has been betrayed. I need time to learn to trust again." She touched a fingertip to his mouth. "This has nothing to do with you. It's my problem. And one I've got to allow myself time to walk through." She held his gaze. "I hope you can understand, but I wouldn't blame you if you didn't."

"If time is what you need to trust in what we have, it's worth the wait for me, Julie," he said. "I love you."

He brushed his lips to hers and she circled her hand behind his neck, drawing him closer, comforted by his presence, comforted by his understanding. "Stay with me," she whispered, looking up to see his dark eyes turn smoky. "I need you with me tonight."

CHAPTER THREE

HANK PEEKED AROUND THE CORNER of the bedroom door and watched Julie sleeping. It was just past dawn and with all the tension and excitement the day before he thought it best not to disturb her.

She stirred and tucked her hand beneath her cheek, cradling it much the same as he'd done more than once last night. A niggling doubt slithered again into his brain. Had what his sister said been true? Was he simply suffering from "white-knight syndrome," trying to swoop in and save Julie? Most men would welcome the delay of being tied down, but despite Julie's assurances, it left a hole deep inside him.

He thought of the weeks he'd planned the proposal, of what her reaction might be. In all of the scenarios, delaying a trip to the altar hadn't been one of them. The conversations—make that arguments—he'd had over the past few months with his sister Caroline teased the already lingering insecurities in his mind.

Two weeks ago, he'd had just one thing left to do—the ring. He'd wanted something special, something different. At the advice of one of his older clients he'd wound up on Michigan Avenue in downtown Chicago, staring up at mighty Atlas shouldering his ancient timepiece over the entrance to Tiffany's.

With the expertise of an older gentleman, Hank had found the perfect bauble. A bright, white Tiffany diamond with two sapphire stones on either side to denote his devotion to her two sons, as well. The matching wedding band was an eternity stone setting of diamonds and sapphires.

Exuberant to share this life-changing moment, he'd called his sister Caroline to see what she thought, and how she thought the parents—who were vacationing in Italy—might react.

He'd invited her to his loft the night before his flight back to Last Hope Ranch, where he'd planned to pop the question while on a sunset flight ending with a celebration dinner at the ranch, compliments of Wyatt and Aimee Kinnison.

He showed the ring to his sister and waited for her squeal of delight.

"Are you *out of your mind*?" She stared at him, eyes wide with alarm.

He glanced at the ring. "What is it? Too much? Not big enough? The guy at Tiffany's said it was a rare design."

"The ring"—Caroline snapped shut the turquoise velvet box, the sound bouncing off the vaulted ceiling like a gunshot—"is exquisite." She sighed, her expression awash with pity. "Henry Adam Richardson, you are a sweet, sweet man. But honey, you've always had this 'knight-in-shining-armor' syndrome." Caroline patted his hand and handed him the box.

"I was...hoping you'd be a bit happier for me, Sis." Hank shook his head. Leave it to his pragmatic sister to see his romantic gesture as something contrived. He placed it on the counter next to the Chicago Dogs take-out sack from their lunch. The jalapenos, usually his favorite, were roiling now in his stomach. "What the hell is 'knight-in-shining-armor' syndrome, anyway?" he asked with a frown.

Caroline rolled her gaze to the ceiling and held her finger up as she took a sip of wine. Hell, if he understood the pairing of Chicago Dogs with wine, but with her, he'd learned to pick his battles. And he had a feeling one was about to commence.

Caroline eyed him. "Let's talk about Samantha McCauley in the third grade.

Had his sister gone bonkers? "You weren't even old enough to remember me in third grade."

"The story, however, is legendary." She held up her hand to silence his refute. "I bet Mother has told the story of her brave and sensitive little boy at least sixty times—maybe more—at dinner parties and family gatherings." She chuckled and took another drink. "Expounding on what a fearless, amazing child you were to jump into the deep end of the pool to rescue little Samantha's hair clip that had fallen to the bottom."

Hank dredged up the old memory and laughed. He took a pull from his beer—by the way, the essential and proper pairing to a Chicago Dog. But he didn't plan to challenge his snotty sister on that point. "I didn't do anything that anyone else wouldn't have done, given the circumstances."

Caroline leaned back, her expression dubious.

"You hadn't even passed your Red Cross lessons yet." She pointed her finger at him. "Then there was that time in fifth grade when Betsy Knight missed the bus and you walked her home."

"Betsy was hot. *That* I do remember." He grinned.

"It was a good thing her daddy brought you back home. The girl lived more than two miles from the school. Lord, when Mother and Father found out what you'd done, they fawned over your brave, courageous heart. You saved that little girl from dangers unknown."

Hank shrugged.

"The thought to call her parents never occurred to you?" Caroline asked.

Hank lifted his beer, took a drink, and then defended himself. "She said her mom would be mad that she missed the bus."

"And why did she miss the bus, big brother?" Caroline peered at him, one dark brow crooked inquisitively. They'd both received their mother's Colombian coloring and hair. Brother and sister were model perfect in looks—Vogue magazine's dream come true. But personality-wise they couldn't have been further apart.

"Kids mess around in the fifth grade," he said.

"I never did," she responded indignantly.

Hank sighed and glanced at his watch. He had a five-a.m. flight time tomorrow and wanted to finish putting his plan together to sweep Julie off her feet.

"The list goes on. You know it as well as I do. The countless times you've rescued the damsel in distress."

WORTH THE WAIT

Hank rolled his eyes and sighed.

"The number of girls who talked your ears off about their boyfriend issues." She raised a pert brow.

He reached up and tugged his earlobes. "Still got 'em."

Caroline looked at him. "I don't want you to get hurt," his sister said with an uncharacteristic softness in her voice. "From what you've told me, that woman has some real issues."

He studied her a moment before answering. "This is the real deal, Sis."

"She almost killed you," Caroline pleaded.

"That was her lunatic ex-husband, not her."

Caroline slumped back in her chair. "It doesn't matter what I say, does it?"

Hank picked up the box, feeling the firm case beneath the velvety softness. It reminded him of the woman he loved. He admired her strength. He loved her mind. Everything else was glorious. Sexy icing on the cake. "Sure it does. But it doesn't change how I feel about Julie." He eyed his sister. "And I hope you'll be happy for us."

Caroline released a weary sigh. "Does this mean I have to attend yet another wedding in that little hick town called End of the Time, Montana?"

"End of the Line," he corrected as he pulled her from the chair and enveloped her in a bear hug.

"Whatever," Caroline muttered. She looked at him with wariness in her gaze. "If she hurts you, just hop in that little plane of yours and come home. Chicago is always here, and this city is filled with plenty of damsels in distress."

"Julie is no damsel, Caroline. She's my queen."

"Okay, I might've just thrown up in my mouth a little." She glanced away and took another sip from her glass.

Hank chuckled and took a pull on his beer. "I know once you get to know her better, you two will be great friends."

She nodded, but her expression belied that she was convinced.

Hank was brought back to the present by Julie's sexy, sleep-induced yawn. She opened her eyes and smiled sleepily. Suddenly, the idea of staying in bed all day appealed to him more than the corporate big-wig and his buddies needing his services to fly them to Arizona for a men's golf weekend.

"You're dressed?" She reached out to him.

Damn. "Julie, it slipped my mind with everything going on yesterday, but I have a client who's asked me to fly him and his buddies to Arizona. I'd drop it in a heartbeat, but the guy's a repeat client—and, I might add, very wealthy. It'd be nice to stash aside for…well, whenever we might need it."

"I see." She leaned up on her elbow. "How long will you be gone?"

"He's scheduled out for ten days. I've got to fly back to Chicago and pick them up. They've hired me to fly them to a couple of Arizona courses, then back to Chicago." The mattress gave as he sat down. Getting too close to her, looking the way she did at the moment, was a dangerous move. "I promise it will go fast."

She slipped her hand in his. "I'll miss you." She offered a sexy pout.

"Yeah?" He grinned. "Maybe you could come with me?"

She sat up, looking snuggly in his T-shirt that she'd slipped on during the night. The old shirt never looked so good. "You know I would if I could, but I have the boys to think of and with all that's going on I don't feel I can just jet off to a week of fun and sun." She grinned as she pulled the shirt over her head, her blond hair tousled and sexy. "Of course, I'll miss you." She leaned forward, captured him around the back of the neck, and drew him into a slow, passionate kiss. Ten seconds more and he'd be calling Alistair Rhoades III to cancel.

He cleared his throat and eased off the bed, looking down at her with a heavy heart and even heavier reservations below his belt. This was, however, a lucrative trip that would set them up nicely for what he hoped would soon be wedding plans. He hated to leave, hated thinking of how well they fit together, her body arched softly against his, of how she seemed so free and trusting in his arms. "This is killing me, babe, but I need to go. I'm meeting this guy at Midway at noon."

Her well-kissed mouth curled into a tempting pout, making him reconsider the money aspect altogether. "Hold that thought…for the next ten days?" He scooped up his jacket and duffel bag.

He stopped suddenly at the door, realizing that Kyle would be leaving for his Scout trip before he returned. "I'll give Kyle a call when I have a moment—tell him to have a good time."

Julie slipped on her robe and smiled. "I appreciate that. It seems the boys are plugged into Uncle Clay and you these days."

Hank shrugged. "It's a guy thing. He'll get over it. Thing is, are you going to be okay?" The urge to walk back and hold her in his arms caused him to grip the door handle a bit tighter.

"I'll be okay. I know it'll be good for him," she said with a soft smile.

"He's going to be fine. They wouldn't take those kids up there if they didn't feel they were ready." Hank glanced at his watch. "I've got to go. See you in a few days."

"Be safe. Call me when you get there," Julie said. "I'll miss you."

Five hours later Hank stood at the private pilot's station at Midway waiting on his client. He'd managed to stop by his loft and grab some clothes and toss a few things out in the fridge that wouldn't survive his absence. Elton John's "The Bitch is Back" ringtone rumbled in his jacket pocket, signaling a call from his sister. He grinned. "Hey, Sis, I was just about to call you before my clients get here."

"You're back in Chicago?" There was a decided enthusiasm, maybe curiosity, in her query.

"Just came back to pick up some guys golfing in Arizona. Hey, I wanted to ask if you'd check on Philly for me?"

"Wait, you're not staying?" she asked. "How did it go? What did she say? What do I tell Mother if she calls?"

WORTH THE WAIT

"Tell her I'll call her later," he said. "And don't forget Philly."

"Hank, I'm not good with plants. You know that. And may I remind you that it's pretty weird that a thirty-two-year-old man names his plants."

"Thanks, Sis." Hank ignored the dig. He spotted Alistair Rhoades walking toward him in stylish-though-heartbreakingly-retro golf slacks in a pale blue and yellow plaid, topped with a canary yellow polo. "Gotta run, Sis."

"But, Hank, you didn't tell me. What did she—"

Hank ended the conversation and stuffed the phone in his pocket as he held his hand out to greet the dashing, silver-haired billionaire. He had no desire to get into the complications of his marriage proposal with his sister.

Hold that thought. Julie had held tight to the memory of smoothing her hands over Hank's incredible body, the thought of how he whispered her name as he brought her to dizzying heights. It had been all she could do *not* to think of it. So much so that in recent days she'd become forgetful. She made excuses for the forgetfulness—work, helping watch the twins, helping with the cabin duties and Frontier Days planning. With half-hearted enthusiasm, she'd shipped her son off on the charter bus carrying a group of Boy Scouts on their first adventure camp to Colorado.

Of course, she'd been thrilled when Hank had suggested Scouts to help her two boys meet new people when they first moved to End of the Line. Chris hadn't quite been ready, sticking close to Julie and befriending Emilee, who was nearly his age, discovering they shared a love for horses. Whatever the reason, she chided herself as she marched through the diner's back room, searching for her notebook which had become her lifeblood of daily lists. She stopped in her tracks as she walked into the diner, her gaze locked on the unexpected stranger.

Had he been more refined, his hair cut shorter, his clothes more polished, he could have been Louis's double. Julie blinked, unable to form any rational thought as she stared blatantly at the man seated next to Dalton at the lunch counter.

Granted, a quick glance around the room proved she was not alone in her assessment and, given the two women with their noses pressed against the front window, she was, in fact, *not* dreaming. Frankly, between Dalton Kinnsion and the new stranger seated beside him, there was very little eating and a lot more slack-jawed staring going on.

Hold onto that thought. Hank's words jumpstarted her brain. Julie gave her head a shake. How ridiculous was she? The man, her ex, had not been who she thought he was. She'd been taken in by his charm and surfer-boy good looks, not knowing a monster lay beneath the surface. Was her judgment so flawed? Could she not see past a shiny façade?

She needed to find her notebook. Julie ducked her head and searched the shelves beneath the counter, hoping to avoid conversation.

"Hey, Julie. Would you mind handing me the coffeepot?" Dalton's request brought her upright.

WORTH THE WAIT

"I don't see Betty around at the moment."

She found herself caught in the steady green-eyed gaze of the stranger. She forced herself to look at Dalton, instead. "Sure." Julie picked up the pot and focused on Dalton's cup.

"Heard Hank had to fly out. When's he due back?" Dalton asked.

Julie heard Dalton talking, but she'd made the mistake of glancing up and catching the smile of the guy next to him.

"That's good, thanks," Dalton said. "Whoa, that's enough." Dalton pulled his cup away before it spilled over the sides.

Hank. Hank loved her. Hank had given her a ring. Told her to hold that thought—just this morning.

"Next week sometime, isn't it?" Betty sidled up beside her and gingerly removed the hot coffeepot from her grasp.

"Uh…Tuesday, I think. I can't seem to remember at the moment," she said with an uneasy laugh.

Dalton eyed her, then glanced over his shoulder. The two women caught at the window gasped and hurried away. Other females in the room went back to eating.

Dalton seemed to realize suddenly what was happening. He tipped his head toward Julie. "Julie Williams, this is Hunter McCoy. Hunter, Julie."

Hunter reached across the counter to shake Julie's hand, and she noticed Dalton turn his head to hide his grin.

"Oh, Julie here is just recently engaged to one of my good friends, Hank Richardson." Dalton offered a smile and a raised brow.

Really? She smiled then at Hunter. "But we haven't set a date yet," she said, holding a firm grasp on her independence. She felt her cheeks heat from the betrayal of emotions warring inside her.

Hey, the guy could be Chris Hemsworth's twin brother—what's a girl to do?

Betty leaned in beside Julie and lowered her voice as she spoke directly to Hunter. "Son," she said with a smile, "you'd best get used to being checked out by the women in this town—single or otherwise." She elbowed Julie playfully. "It's not often we get someone who looks like…oh, who is that guy from the comic book movies?"

"Thor," Dalton, Julie, and Hunter said at the same time.

Julie looked at the stranger and he flashed her a charming grin. He wore a faded olive-drab shirt stretched tightly over a broad chest that left little to imagine of the chiseled muscle beneath. His dirty blond hair, streaked by the sun, hung past his shoulders, and his blue-green eyes seemed aware of everything around him.

"I get that a lot, *sans* the accent, of course," he said. Hunter offered Betty a bashful grin, making him all the more adorable. His voice was pleasant, smooth like the breeze on a summer's evening. "I just finished portraying Wild Bill Hickok down in Deadwood this summer. Filled in for a buddy of mine. Since I got back stateside, I haven't given much thought to cutting my hair. I guess it worked for Wild Bill—why not me?" He glanced at Dalton. "Hey, but I *am* really glad this guy came along when he did. Wasn't sure how far I was going to have to walk to find a town." He offered Betty a white, even grin. "But I'd sure walk a mile to eat a breakfast like this again, Betty," he said, dropping Julie's hand to pick up Betty's.

Julie had never seen Betty blush, but this man brought pink to her friend's cheeks.

"Need that coffee warmed up?" Betty asked, holding up the coffeepot over Hunter's cup.

"Thank you, ma'am. I'd appreciate that." He held out his cup. "I had some business in Billings and was on my way here, actually, when my old truck broke down. This guy"—he slapped Dalton's shoulder—"was kind enough to pick me up and get me a tow."

"Nan's got to order in the parts for that classic truck," Dalton said, and turned back to Julie. "I thought maybe he could stay down at the cabins until his truck is repaired. You don't happen to know if anything is currently open?" Dalton asked.

"Things are pretty full right now, except..." She hesitated with what she was about to offer. Then again, Hank spent more time in her cabin than he did his, so perhaps he wouldn't mind. Besides, odds were that his truck would be repaired and Hunter on his way before Hank returned, anyway.

"You could bunk at Hank's cabin for a couple of days. At least, until another cabin opens." Julie admonished the odd flutters in her stomach, chalking it up to scattered emotions.

Dalton hesitated, then held his cup out for Betty to refill. "You're sure Hank wouldn't mind?"

She started to explain, but chose to keep their intimate lives private. "I can't see that he'd mind. 'Course, you'll need fresh linens. There's another set at the cabin, I'm sure." She went back to searching for her wayward notebook, determined to avoid any more interactions with this man than was absolutely necessary. "But you should probably give Wyatt a call and let him know about the arrangements."

"Of course," Hunter said. "I'll want to pay for my stay."

"Okay, then," Dalton said. "I'll give Wyatt a call and take you on down to the ranch." He looked past Hunter at two women who he'd noticed had been lingering at the register for several minutes. "You gave Nan your cell number, right?"

Hunter nodded and slid off the barstool.

"Probably should get you outta here," Dalton said, smirking, "before you create a mob scene."

"Thank you for your hospitality, Julie" Hunter said.

"Yes, indeed," Betty muttered quietly as she walked behind Julie.

Jarred by Betty's comment, Julie smiled. "You're welcome, Mr. McCoy. Excuse me"—she spotted the notebook under a pile of folded towels—"but I need to get back to work."

"It was nice to meet you," he said, the smooth-as-whiskey tone of his voice causing gooseflesh to rise on her arms.

She turned and offered a smile and a nod.

Her eyes widened when he offered a quick wink. Confused, she shook off what her mind fleetingly perceived as flirtatious behavior. She admonished herself mentally. She knew nothing at all about this man—his backstory, if he had a wife and kids. Though she'd happened to notice he wasn't wearing a ring.

But *she* was. What kind of newly engaged woman would notice such a thing? She ducked her head and hurried to the back room.

Julie felt her phone vibrate in her pocket and, seeing it was Hank, looked for a bit of privacy to take the call. "Taking this outside in the alley," she told Jerry, who was flipping pancakes on the griddle.

"Hey, you," she said, walking out the back door, "tell me again, when you're coming home?" She parked herself on the low concrete wall against the landscaped hill leading up to the newly added outdoor patio. It had been designed and built by Rein and Liberty Mackenzie as a gift to Betty and Jerry on the diner's twenty-fifth anniversary.

With the launch of MacKenzie's online decorating and custom furniture business, End of the Line had been catapulted into a vibrant tourist destination in recent months. And with Frontier Days coming up in a few weeks, the area hotels, cabins, bed-and-breakfasts, and even the campground had been booked in full in anticipation of the town's events.

"Well, that's nice to hear," Hank said. "I miss you, too. You still holding on to that thought?"

"I am," Julie said, though admittedly with a small amount of confusion and guilt rattling around inside. "I have been. It's been quite a week already. Sending Kyle off, Frontier Days looming on the horizon, my accounting work, plus I've been trying to help out more with the cabins, given Aimee's condition. She's not due for another month, but she seems to be having a tougher time with keeping up her energy level." Somewhere in the back of her mind, Julie realized she was rambling. "Rebecca has been helping, and the kids, too, when Michael doesn't need them."

"Whew. Wow, honey, take a breath," Hank said. "Everything will work out. One day at a time, okay?"

"Yeah, I know. I'm sorry to ramble like that. It's just that you know how I get when I commit to something." The minute the words were out she regretted them. It seemed, and rightly so, that she was committed to everyone and everything around her, with the exception of the wedding date. "I'm sorry, I didn't mean to imply—"

"No worries, honey. I understand." His tender tone calmed her. She needed to speak with him about Hunter staying at his place.

Voices up the hill caught her attention and she turned to find her gaze locked with the new stranger in town—the man she'd given permission to sleep in Hank's bed.

She leapt to her feet and hurried inside. Seeing the restroom door open, she hurried inside, turned on the light, and shut the door. "Sorry, too much noise outside."

"No problem. Same here. Listen, honey, I wanted to talk with you about something."

"I need to talk with you, too," she said, leaning against the small vanity. "You go ahead."

"Okay. These guys have made an offer to pay me double to fly them out to San Diego for a few extra days. It's good money, but I wanted to get your thoughts. If the timing is bad, I can tell them no."

Julie turned and looked at her reflection in the mirror. *Come home.* Given her treacherous thoughts in the past few moments, she found it difficult to speak.

"You still there?" he asked. "Listen, I can tell them no in a heartbeat. I can be home day after tomorrow."

"No," she interjected with more force than necessary. "You're right. The money will go a long way to help with the wedding." She pushed a hand through her hair. She wasn't sure if he'd even told his parents yet. He'd taken her and the boys to Chicago for Christmas last year and the weekend hadn't proved to be the best. She'd gotten the impression that she and her boys weren't what they had in mind for their only son. Not that there was any hurry, since no date had been set. "I've got so much going on anyway. No, you go on ahead and stay."

There was a brief silence.

"You're sure?" he asked.

She heard the odd uncertainty in his voice and it twisted her insides. "Absolutely." *Not at all.* But I have to find out.

"Okay, then, if you're sure. It really is pretty amazing what they're offering," he said. "Now, what'd you need to tell me?"

Julie opened her mouth to answer and someone pounded on the door. "I just...miss you." That much was true. It was easy when he was around. He took care of her, gave her everything she wanted. But was that enough? Enough to last a lifetime?

"It won't be long and when I get back, I'll do

whatever you need me to do to help, okay?"

She knew he'd cut off his right arm to be there if she told him she needed him. The choice was hers. She could tell him to come home and she wouldn't have to face whatever this unexpected attraction was with this stranger in town, or she could deal with it alone and confirm it once and for all—her love for Hank, body and soul. "You're so good to me," she said, turning away from the mirror so she wouldn't have to look into her own eyes.

"You know I love being there for you," Hank said.

"Hank, wait." Julie opened her mouth to explain about Hunter staying at his place. But she knew he'd change his plans and fly home, and so she decided against it. She would handle this, and in so doing prove to herself that what she felt for Hank was the real McCoy.

She cringed at the analogy. "Be safe. I'll see you in a few days."

"Yes, and when I get home, we're going to take a day or two and I'll show you how much I missed you."

Julie had no doubt he would, and the thought both warmed and confused her at the same time. The only man she'd dated since her divorce was Hank. Finding another man attractive wasn't a sin, but doing something about it…she would risk losing everything. "Hank, I—"

"Hank. Come on over here," a voice called in the background.

"Honey, I've got to go, Alistair wants me to meet someone," Hank said. "I love you."

Perhaps she'd just text him later. Julie shook her head. Nothing was going to happen. She was almost certain of it. "Okay, I—" the words caught in her throat. "I'll see you in a few days."

There was a brief pause and the line disconnected.

CHAPTER FOUR

HANK SAT IN HIS CONDO overlooking the golf course. He envisioned bringing Julie and the boys to the posh resort. Though he wasn't into golf that much, he was able to fantasize about lounging by the pool with Julie, followed by a couple's massage. He'd take them all on a family excursion to Rawhide where they'd eat from a chuckwagon and dance to music under the stars. He glanced at his phone and thought of calling Julie, but after their last conversation decided to give her some space. She'd sounded overwhelmed. Not surprising given her accounting work for both the diner and the bakery, chairing the committees for the Frontier Days celebration, and helping out now and then with her twin nieces to give Clay and Sally time to breathe. It was no great wonder that she didn't want to set a wedding date. If there was one thing he knew well about Julie, it was her fierce dedication to whatever she made a commitment to. That should probably be enough to ease his concerns, given she'd said that she wanted to marry him…eventually. Instead, it left a niggling seed of doubt in his mind. She trusted him with certain things, such as asking if he'd call Kyle in a couple of days to see how he was doing. She hadn't wanted her son to feel like she was being overprotective. Hank had agreed, appreciating that at least she seemed to entrust him with her sons.

Kyle had sounded oddly relieved to hear Hank's voice. "Hey, Hank. Thanks for calling."

"Hey, buddy. Thought I'd give you a quick call and see how things are going." He remembered when Kyle had first arrived at the ranch. Sullen, quiet, he lashed out at his mom, at Hank, at nearly anyone who tried to be kind to him. His experience at school that first year had been on shaky ground, as well. There'd been several visits to the principal's office to discuss Kyle's aggressive behavior until a young teacher, a recent transplant from Georgia, came to the middle school to speak about sports and how disciplined and focused you needed to be. That, and spending many hours with his Uncle Clay, had done much to help the boy see beyond his anger.

But, as was stated in the settlement, once every three months Julie was bound to take the boys to see their father in a supervised prison visit. Hank would fly them out and wait outside the room during those visits, but each time Kyle would backslide into his anger afterward. Seeing a flyer in town one day, Hank had suggested Julie enroll the boys in the local Scout troop, just so they could meet other kids their age. Kyle had taken to the challenges naturally, taking an interest in the technological aspects, and Chris found his interests in being outdoors, specifically around the horses and his good friend, Emilee Kinnison.

"Yeah, we just arrived at the main campground yesterday. It's pretty cool. We got to stop and see some neat stuff like Crazy Horse and Mount Rushmore."

Hank listened, patient in letting the boy give an account for what seemed like every mile of the bus trip. "Wow, sounds like you've had quite a time and you've only just gotten to the adventure camp. It sounds like you're having some amazing experiences. I bet your mom would like to know you're having such a great time."

"Yeah," he said, sounding evasive. "Maybe you could tell her when you talk to her?" Kyle hurried to add, "I'm not sure how good my signal is out here."

"Or maybe you could call her now, knowing you have a signal?" Hank suggested.

"Yeah," Kyle lowered his voice. "The thing is, nobody else has called their parents, you know?"

Hank realized then that Kyle was one of the younger Scouts on the trip and was probably trying to be like the older guys. He heard loud voices and laughter in the background.

"Hey, Hank, I gotta go, okay?"

"Sure thing, buddy. Have fun. Stay—" The line disconnected. "Safe."

That had been a day or so ago and he'd let Julie know Kyle was doing fine and why he hadn't called.

"One of those guy things, right?" she'd asked.

"Exactly," Hank had assured her.

"Thanks, babe, I appreciate you," she'd told him. It wasn't "I love you," but he'd take it.

Hank's cell phone rang, jarring him from his thoughts. It was Rein MacKenzie.

"Hey, Rein. What's going on?" Hank asked,

pleased to detour his mind from going down a dark path of concern about his fiancée.

"Not too bad. Liberty's almost finished with the nursery. Aimee's in great health. Plans for Frontier Days are clicking along thanks to Julie's organizational skills. The woman's a dynamo," Rein said.

"That she is," Hank agreed.

"Listen, I'm helping Justin with the rodeo. You remember we talked about it a bit the other night at dinner? That's one of the reasons I'm calling."

"Sure, what do you need?" Hank asked.

"I wanted to ask if you'd like to be one of our rodeo sponsors—that is, your charter flight business," Rein continued. "We've got Dusty's Bar and Grill on board and Wyatt's putting up an ad for the Last Hope Ranch cabin rentals and the Equine Rescue Stables. I've just started gathering our sponsorships, but I have a feeling it's not going to be hard to do. We have twenty-five slots at five-hundred a piece and you get a professional banner with your name and logo that we'll tie on the fence around the perimeter of the arena. What do you say?"

Hank chuckled. "A banner? Heck, who can say no to that. Sign me up."

"Great, I appreciate your support," Rein said.

"How are the preparations coming? I've been curious how Justin plans to pull this together," Hank asked, wishing he was there to roll up his sleeves and help out.

"We've been hauling in and repairing some of the old school bleachers they'd stored in the bus garage. They aren't pretty, but they're sturdy and will work to make seating. The best part is, the school donated them to the event."

Hank looked out over the lush, green golf course and thought of the burnished gold hayfields and snowcapped purple mountains that surrounded End of the Line. Growing up in Chicago, he'd never thought his heart would feel the sense of freedom under expansive blue skies; never realized how the call of an owl in the dead of night could bring him peace. Lying next to Julie might have much to do with that, as well.

"We're going to have mutton busting, junior barrel riding, and amateur bronc riding. Maybe tractor pulls, if we can get enough entrants."

"Sounds like fun." Hank shifted in the club chair overlooking the resort. It was a balmy ninety-eight in the desert shade, but from where he sat, it was a pleasant seventy degrees. "I'm sorry I'm not there to help out."

"You and me both," Rein said. "Hey, but you could always ante up and ride a bronc. The purse is going to a good cause."

Hank laughed. "Let me check to see if my insurance is up to date."

"You'd be doing a good deed," Rein said. "Another, at any rate, to add to your list."

Hank swirled the cubes in his glass of iced tea. He thought back to his conversation with Julie. She'd mentioned nothing about any good deeds. Maybe Rein had misunderstood what he'd heard. "I haven't done much of anything yet, other than the banner, but I will look at things when I get back."

"No, I'm talking about the guy staying at your place," Rein said.

Hank leaned forward in the chair. Did he say there was a guy staying in his cabin? "Yeah? I don't think I heard about this."

"Oops, I figured you and Julie had already discussed it. Sorry, man. I ran into Dalton and he mentioned the situation."

"Situation?" Hank asked.

"Yeah, why the guy is staying at your cabin for a couple of days."

Hank stood and stared out the sliding doors leading to his second-story balcony. "Yeah, who is this *guy* and how does Dalton know him?"

"Dalton said the guy's truck broke down between here and Billings. Dalton picked him up and they towed his truck to Nan's. Guess it's a classic truck. She had to order parts and it could be a couple of days."

Hank rubbed his hand over his mouth and released a quiet sigh. Never mind that this guy was living in his cabin, but Julie hadn't even bothered to mention that fact to him.

"Hey, I hope I didn't open a can of worms," Rein said.

Hank's gaze narrowed on movement in the limb of a tree. A large bird seemed to be peering at him. Was it a falcon? "So, Dalton doesn't know this guy really well?" He squinted at the massive bird, confused—he could've sworn it was a snowy owl. The American Indian lore about the great owl appearing before an impending storm drifted into his brain. That, of course, was entirely absurd—this was Arizona, not Montana. Then again "impending storm" could simply be a metaphor for many different things. That didn't ease his mind any.

"I'm just curious as to what anybody knows about this guy who is sleeping in my bed?" Hank tried to reel in the frustration building inside. Maybe Dalton had made the decision himself, knowing that he was gone this week. "Does Julie know?"

Rein cleared his throat. "Uh, she was the one who suggested it."

Ouch. So much for that theory. "I see."

"Look, he's ex-Army Ranger. He's from Texas, taking care of his father's last wishes to have his ashes scattered at a number of bucket list places, apparently."

"And End of the Line was one of them?" Hank searched the liquor tray, found the whiskey, and poured a liberal finger into his tea glass. He tossed it down quickly, hardly aware of the slow burn sliding down his throat.

"No, his dad was adopted, born in Billings. Somehow he found records that indicated that the woman who gave birth to his dad might have lived around here."

"I wonder what he had to do to get that information," Hank muttered, not masking his sarcasm. The guy was likely a war hero, loved his country. *The original Boy Scout.* Always ready to perform a good deed. The idea that Julie suggested it without even consulting him exacerbated his concerns.

"Well, I know Dalton wouldn't have picked him up if he didn't think the guy's story was legit," Rein offered.

"Ex-Army Ranger?"

"That's what Dalton said."

WORTH THE WAIT

"And Julie offered him the cabin?"

"That, you'll have to take up with her. In all fairness to her, man, you live at her place ninety percent of the time," Rein said.

"Yeah." Rein had a point, but why wouldn't Julie just tell him?

"Hey, I've got to finish more calls. We've got pens to build this afternoon. Thanks again for the sponsorship. We'll settle up when you get home. And, uh...sorry if I spoke out of turn. Julie has so much going on that I'm sure she didn't think it was a big deal. The guy is only here until Nan gets his truck fixed. Literally everything else is booked up."

"Sure. Hey, give Liberty my best. See you guys in a few days." Hank dropped the phone on the table. Maybe he'd moved too fast. He glanced at the phone, picked it up, and dialed Dalton.

"Hey, trouble. What's going on?" Dalton answered.

"Not much. Had a call from Rein today."

"He hit you up for the rodeo sponsorship?" Dalton asked.

"Yeah, I'm happy to help out. But that's not why I'm calling."

"Okay, shoot, but be warned, I'm playing single dad while Angie is in town with Rebecca," Dalton said.

"I wanted to know more about this guy staying at my place."

There was a brief silence.

"You mean Hunter?"

"Are there more men staying at my place than I'm aware of?" Hanks asked.

He heard Dalton sigh. "No, man. Hunter is a guy I picked up just outside of town. His truck broke down—"

"Yeah, Rein mentioned that."

"He's on a mission to fulfill his father's dying wish to find his birth mom. Billings hospital records indicated a Jane Doe from End of the Line. 'Course, that was in a different time."

"Sure. Sounds like small town drama is alive and well," Hank said. Over the years, End of the Line had become like a second home. So, too, had the trials and tribulations of life in the once-booming gold mining town. Nowadays, all traces of the gold rush were overgrown with weeds and filled in with rock. Only a couple of actual mines still existed, but were boarded up with "no trespassing" signs.

"So, has he had any luck finding his grandmother?"

"Not yet. Nan had to order parts for his dad's old truck. Classic ride, but he's been driving the thing all over the country spreading his dad's ashes—"

"Yeah, Rein mentioned that, too. Sounds morbid, if you ask me. And *you* feel comfortable letting him stay next door to Julie and the boys?"

"And my brother and his pregnant wife up the road, not to mention the other guests." Dalton paused. "What's going on, Hank?"

Hank realized that he'd allowed Julie's delay in setting a date spill over into a host of uncertainties.

"Are you and Julie—" Dalton left the sentence open.

"We're fine. I think. She just forgot to mention

that she'd offered my cabin to this guy."

"Ah, I see." Dalton said. "And you don't think it's because you aren't here and when you are, you're at her place? When was the last time you slept in that cabin, by the way?"

Hank sighed. It was true. He'd allowed himself to imagine the worst.

"Besides," Dalton said, "you've got nothing to worry about. Just because the guy looks like Thor and creates sighs from women on the street—"

"You're an A-hole, you know that," Hank said, but with a grin. He knew his friend was poking fun at him. Still, thinking of a guy like that living next door to Julie didn't settle well. Especially given her desire to explore her new-found freedom.

"So, aren't you back soon, anyway?" Dalton asked.

"Yeah, well, these guys offered me quite a chunk of change if I'd stay on for a few more days and fly them to a resort in southern California to play a course there."

"Rough life," Dalton said. "So, you'll be back… oh lord, hang on a sec." The phone thudded to a surface and, in the background, he heard Dalton gently reprimand Sawyer. "We talked about this, son. The puppy doesn't need your pacifier. And you don't eat his dog treats."

There was the sound of scuffling, followed by a high-pitched, defiant squeal. Dalton returned momentarily "Sorry, Sawyer has decided that trading his pacifier for the dog's treat biscuit is a fair deal."

Hank had never been around kids that small.

Not that he hadn't thought of him and Julie adding another child to their family some day. Hell, he had to get her convinced to set a date, much less have another child.

"Hey, extending a few days sounds like a lucrative deal, if Julie's good with it," Dalton said, then whispered harshly to his young son, clearly distracted.

"You go take care of your family. I'll see you in a few days, unless these guys decide to call it quits," Hank said.

"Okay, man. Hey, take care and seriously, don't worry," Dalton said. "I know the whole engagement thing kind of got off on a rocky start, but Julie loves you. That's clear to everyone."

Except she hasn't said those words to me yet. "Give your family a squeeze from Uncle Hank."

"You bet," Dalton said, and hung up.

Julie dug through the myriad boxes covered in thick dust. She brushed away the cobwebs and held her forearm to her face to stifle a sneeze.

"My stars and garters," she heard Nan say from behind a barrier of old furniture piled against one another reaching to the attic's ceiling. "I should have warned you about the dust. I haven't been up here in years."

In an attempt to delegate the responsibilities of the Frontier Days celebration, Julie had accepted Nan's offer to organize the veterans' float for the community parade.

Though Nan kept busy running Patuzky Sporting Goods and Repair as well as caring for her best friend, Gwen, a resident at the End of the Line nursing home, she loved being involved in community efforts. She and her late husband, Andy, had often spearheaded various community projects in years past.

Julie coughed in the wake of not one, but at least three consecutive sneezes. On this Saturday morning, she'd agreed to help Nan find her husband's box containing his uniform and other articles from his service in Vietnam.

Julie was grateful for the help. Taking on the responsibility of chairman of the Frontier Days celebration had been a way to help ease into community involvement, planting some roots. She and Hank had never broached the subject of the future. She was happy to live in the present. Each day had taught her something new about herself. She'd just begun to grasp that freedom, to enjoy being with a man who required no legalities to maintain their relationship.

Then he'd proposed, and everything went sideways. She loved finding out who she was, but she knew that Hank loved her and her boys and he wanted more—he wanted the whole package.

"Good heavens," Nan called out.

Julie hoisted herself to her feet with the aid of an old sea trunk and gingerly stepped over piles of books and sundry items. "Did you find something?" she asked, peeking around the corner of an old dresser, vanity, and headboard. She found Nan seated on the floor, a battery-operated lantern placed in a chair beside her for light. She was surrounded by stacks of magazines, old records, and what appeared to be postcards. A box lay open in front of her. She carefully pulled out a jacket from its cardboard prison, unfolding it with reverence as she held it up into the light. Several pins above the breast pocket winked in the new light. Nan smiled as she turned to look up at Julie. "You know, I can remember the day he stepped off the bus in this uniform. He looked so sharp. And even though I'd been actively against the war, I was never prouder to be in that crowd welcoming him and the other men in town home." She chuckled quietly. "It's true what they say about a man in uniform." She looked back, eyeing the now musty-smelling garment. "I couldn't wait to get him out of the darn thing." Nan glanced up at Julie. "Sorry if I'm being too forward. But I'm guessing you may have felt that way about a certain pilot from Chicago from time to time."

Julie smiled, skirting effectively around her comment. "I can't imagine what it was like having him so far away, not knowing the dangers he faced."

Nan nodded. "It was every bit as bad as they said it was. And frankly, we'll never know how bad it was. We wrote often. Andy told me I was his lifeline to the sane world. Even though we'd broken off our relationship, I still cared deeply for him. We were barely out of high school when we broke up. I was looking to go to college. He wanted to get married. Not long after, he moved to Billings to work, and a few months later I found out he'd enlisted. He didn't tell me right away. He knew I'd taken a stand against the war. But eventually I started receiving letters from him and I answered them, finding myself falling in love with him all

WORTH THE WAIT

over again."

"Did you keep those letters?" Julie asked.

"I've got them stored downstairs in a lockbox," she said. With a curious look, she ruffled deeper into the box. "I wonder if he kept mine."

Julie was drawn to Nan's story. "When did you know you...for sure...that *he* was the one, the one you wanted to marry?"

Nan sighed. "I think I learned more about myself in those years apart. The war took its toll on everyone." She pulled out a hat and brushed her bony fingers across the brim. "Two weeks after he returned, I was the one to ask him to marry me."

Julie grinned. "Really?"

Nan nodded. "This progressive little hippie had decided she didn't want anyone else on this journey, so I gave him back the ring he'd once used to propose to me and asked him to marry me."

"Wow, that's quite a story, Nan," Julie said.

"Nicholas Sparks stuff, right?" Nan laughed. Her gaze narrowed. "You having doubts about your engagement?"

Julie averted her gaze from the old woman. Her inability to set a wedding date and the high school way she'd reacted to Hunter McCoy had rattled her. Questions ate away at her. What if the feelings she had for Hank weren't real? What if her feelings for Hank were no more than an overblown sense of gratitude? I mean, how many men would be willing to take on a woman and two adolescent boys scarred by such a horrible trauma? Would she have many other choices? "How'd you know you loved him?" she asked, meeting met

Nan's steady gaze.

"I'm not sure that's the same for everyone, sweetheart. For me, it was knowing that when we were apart, I felt empty." She looked at the hat. "Love always seems to find a way, despite our choices."

Julie swallowed, wondering whether she should put off marrying Hank. He was an attractive, kind-hearted man who any woman in her right mind would want. Maybe being married to Louis had broken her, created something inside her that made her feel undeserving of a man like Hank. "Did you have children?" she asked, wanting to change the subject.

Nan shrugged, her smile brave. "Doctors said I wasn't able. So, we started our business here, did a little traveling. Got involved in the community. It was enough, I guess."

Julie frowned. "You guess?"

"Well, I'd always dreamt of having kids," Nan said. "But we often did things for the school and had our annual children's fishing trip where we taught kids to fly fish. That's where I first met those Kinnison boys and Rein. Jed sent them to us that first summer after their mom left Wyatt and Dalton. Thought it'd be good for them. Turned out, those boys were naturals. Eventually we had them come help us with the expeditions."

Julie listened, searching the eyes of a woman married for over fifty years to the same man. There was a certainty in her gaze, a camaraderie that still existed even though he'd passed on. Their life, it seemed, had been a partnership.

"Why don't we take this downstairs before we

WORTH THE WAIT

inhale too much more of this dust," Nan said, handing the cap and jacket to Julie.

She folded the flaps of the box shut and lifted it from its hidden existence on the bottom shelf. "We'll see if there's anything else the old man tucked away that we might be able to use."

Julie stood and held out her hand. "Do you need some help up?"

Nan laughed. "At almost seventy-four, I can use all the help I can get, sweet pea." She gripped Julie's hand and rose to her feet.

A few moments later, Julie had put on a pot of coffee while Nan began removing items from the box on the kitchen table.

"Oh, look, he did save them." Nan pulled a stack of yellowed letters tied with twine from the box. As though lost in the past, she untied the string and began sifting through, checking the dates.

Julie set a cup of coffee in front of her and sat down across the table, silent as she watched the woman trek down memory lane.

A frown marred Nan's pleasant expression. Laying the other letters aside, she focused on one in particular, sliding the letter from its opened envelope.

She watched the emotions pass through the old woman's eyes as she read the letter. "Nan, are you okay?" Julie asked.

A small sigh escaped her lips, and then Nan rested her hand to her forehead. For a moment Julie said nothing, allowing Nan to process whatever it was that had so obviously affected her. "Nan?" Julie asked again.

"It was all a lie," Nan said softly.

Julie covered the old woman's hand, offering comfort for what she could see was difficult news. "What do you mean, it was all a lie?"

Nan's eyes—as alone and sad as Julie had ever felt or seen—met her gaze. She handed the letter to Julie and stared out the kitchen window.

"He had a son," Nan said.

"What?" Julie frowned.

"Read it."

Julie saw the note was addressed to Andy, Nan's husband.

Dear Andy,

It has been years since we last spoke. I hope you and Nan are doing well. You two were meant for each other and that is why I hesitated to tell you the truth about that night we had in Billings. I knew then that while you'd broken off your engagement, your heart still belonged to Nan. But you were off to war and I suppose we needed one another's comfort.

But the truth is, I had a child. Yours, and because I was unmarried and you were at war, I felt I had no recourse but to give the child up for adoption.

Why would I tell you this now? All these years later? It is because I have been diagnosed with Alzheimer's and I want to move back home and be buried next to my parents in my hometown.

I never saw him. Never held our son. How could I? This was a baby that should have been yours and Nan's. I swear my intentions were good. I only ever wanted you two to be happy. I hope that you and Nan might find it possible in your hearts to one day forgive me."

It was simply signed, *"Gwen."*

"Who's Gwen?" Julie asked, folding the one letter and carefully placing it back in its yellowing

WORTH THE WAIT

envelope.

"My best friend," Nan said. "She moved back to End of the Line more than ten years ago." She placed her palm to her forehead and shook her head.

"Nan?"

"Read the second letter," she said quietly.

Julie found the other envelope and opened the letter. This one was written by Nan's late husband several years ago.

My dearest Nan,

Should you ever choose to delve into this box filled only with things related to my serving in the military (a time not at the top of your priority list, I'm sure!) I want you to understand why I chose not to mention my short-lived affair with Gwen, or the surprising news she shared, I surmise, out of her own guilty conscience these many years later. I blame myself for her grief. I was not entirely fair to her, I fear. For only one woman had captured my heart, even when you and I had parted. But she was sweet and kind, and the comfort she offered riddled me with guilt. That is, in part, why I chose to enlist. At the time, I needed to get away from anything and anyone that reminded me of us.

I never knew of this child until the date of this letter. I was angry with Gwen at first for waiting so long to tell me, but realized that she'd done what was best for the child. That's what is important here. By now, he'd be into his twenties—well over half our married life together. Happy (I trust!) in our business, our home, our town, and the life we'd chosen. I didn't feel it would do anyone any good in our present life to dredge up the past. My hope is that whoever adopted this child did right by him and gave him a good life. The kind of life that neither Gwen nor myself at the time could have given him. It isn't as though I don't think of him, and in some way, even love him, perhaps. But I wasn't his real father—not the man who carried him to bed, talked to him about girls, watched him graduate. Those are another man's memories and well deserved. Mine are about us, the life we made together, and I've never regretted a single moment.

Perhaps one day after you read this, you can forgive me. But understand this—I loved the life we had and I've never loved anyone but you."

It was signed, "*Yours, Andy.*"

"Oh, Nan," Julie said.

Nan lifted her palm to Julie. "I'm fine, or I will be once I process this. It's far easier to forgive someone who's already gone." She looked at Julie. "The greater challenge is forgiving your best friend. Seeing her every Sunday afternoon. Watching her memory these past ten years drift in and out of reality." She shook her head. "I can forgive the indiscretion. I had turned down Andy's proposal. We weren't together. They found each other before he was to ship out."

"But she's never mentioned any of this"—Julie held up the letter—"to you?"

Nan shook her head and sucked in a ragged breath. "Not a word. The Alzheimer's has ravaged her memory. Most days she has no idea who I am. Only a kind lady who brings her gumdrops from the five and dime. The staff says that when I'm gone she sits by the window and stares at the butterfly garden outside."

"I don't know what to say." Julie squeezed Nan's hand. This kind of news at any age would be a sucker punch to the gut, but at Nan's age and given the circumstances, Julie was at a loss for words.

"What is there to say?" Nan shrugged.

Julie attempted to reason with her. "You and your husband were very happy. Perhaps, since it had happened so long ago, he felt it unnecessary to tell you."

"Not necessary to tell me that he'd had a child with my best friend?" Nan clamped her hand over her chest. "What kind of man does that?"

"A man who had no idea that he was a father," Julie reminded her.

"But marriage is built on trust," Nan said. "There shouldn't be secrets between you. If there is a difficult situation, you face it together."

Her words struck home. She and Hank weren't married but she'd purposely kept news from him that she felt wasn't necessary for him to know. "Nan, your marriage wasn't a lie. You guys had a full life. You told me about it. And you had each other. You had a true partner in every sense of the word. He didn't want to hurt you with news that by then wouldn't have made any difference in your lives."

Her gaze lifted to Julie's "But I might have a stepson out there, maybe step-grandchildren by now."

Julie's heart twisted for the loss Nan felt.

"I know. I'm sorry. I wish there was something I could say or do." Julie stood and walked behind the woman seated at the table. She leaned down and wrapped her arms around Nan. The tough-as-nails woman, usually dressed in baggy bib overalls, a T-shirt, and red bandana wrapped around her short silvery hair, seemed to have aged before Julie's eyes. "It's going to be okay. You'll see." She stepped back and regarded her friend. "Nan, I'd completely understand if you'd rather not be involved with the veterans' float."

Nan cleared her throat and squared her shoulders. She shook her head as though dispelling the dark thoughts. "No, you're right. Andy and the other vets, they deserve this float in recognition for their service. That's what is important here." She stood and walked to the kitchen window. "It has nothing to do with my personal issues." She glanced back at Julie. "I just need time to think about what to say to Gwen." She shrugged. "Or if I should say anything at all."

"If she doesn't remember you, Nan, what would be the point?" Julie asked.

The old woman rested her hands on the kitchen counter. "Forgiveness, I suppose. Saying aloud that I forgive her would be helpful to me." She looked at Julie. "Does that sound selfish?"

"Not at all, but it comes with a certain amount of risk. She may not understand."

Nan nodded. "I've been visiting her every Sunday for over ten years. Some days she looks at me and I swear she knows me. Most days, I'm a pleasant distraction from her silence."

Julie felt for both women. She wasn't certain that under similar circumstances she'd be as gracious. "You are a remarkable and courageous woman, Nan." She lifted her bookbag over her shoulder. "I'm going to head back to work and give you time to think through things. Our meeting is tomorrow after the lunch rush in the party room."

"I'll be there," Nan said. "I need to go see Gwen, but I'll be there."

CHAPTER FIVE

SITTING BY A SPARKLING AZURE pool surrounded by palm trees and exotic tropical gardens with a spectacular ocean view, Hank decided it wasn't the worst way to spend a day. He sat back and adjusted his Ray-Bans. Currently, he was the only one poolside, giving him the freedom to imagine Julie in a sleek black swimsuit gliding through the water, emerging with a smile that suggested the afternoon delights awaiting them back in their room.

The sound of male laughter followed promptly by a wheezing cough jarred him from his hot little daydream, but not so his need for the woman he loved. Would there ever be a time when he tired of her? The soft scent of her skin, the warmth of her unhurried touch, the way she searched his eyes after they made love. They had no issues in the physical sense, but there were far deeper scars he could only imagine that she struggled with—the least of which were betrayal, fear, and mistrust. If anything, he should count his blessings that their relationship had lasted this long.

He understood what it meant to wait. From the time he'd met her his senior year of college, he'd waited for her to notice him. Even years later,

WORTH THE WAIT

when she'd moved away with another man, he'd pined for her, pushing aside the guilt as well as his broken heart to move forward with his life. Then two years ago, fate placed her in his path again. He intended to hang on this time, but that didn't make the waiting any less excruciating.

A warm coastal breeze brushed his cheek as he glanced at his phone, tempted to call and ask why she hadn't told him about lending the stranger his house for a few days. It was petty, perhaps, but at a time when trust seemed to be a key component in their relationship, Hank figured it went both ways. He placed the phone on the table, face down, telling himself not to be so paranoid. To show her that he trusted her.

"Hank? Hank Richardson?"

A chill ran across his shoulders. Years melted away. Memories, and not all of them entirely sane, leapt to the forefront of his mind, obliterating all other thoughts.

Hank looked up. Standing like a statuesque Grecian goddess in a slinky, low-cut black jumpsuit, was Cynthia Simmons, two years his senior, and in college had been captain of the Northwestern dance squad. She was also the only daughter of Gerald Simmons, Dean of the College of Arts and Sciences. She'd been the only woman in the world who had existed to him for the span of a few weeks in his sophomore year.

Hank blinked a couple of times and found his tongue. "What the heck are you doing here?" He laughed his query off as a joke, but glanced around, concerned about whether her father might also be nearby. He'd spent the greater share of his college career avoiding direct contact with the dean, certain he'd face immediate expulsion for all the times he'd snuck out after midnight into their grand home just a block off campus.

"What? Not even a hug?" She opened her arms, a gesture he remembered on a most intimate level. "Really? After all we've shared?"

His water glass wobbled precariously as he stood in haste to greet her. She pressed against him, still wearing the same perfume that had driven him mad back in college. He stepped away quickly and cleared his throat. "Are you in town on business?" He remembered that she'd been a business major.

"As a matter of fact, my husband and I own this resort," she said with a shrug, "And a couple of others up the coast." She peered at him with a curious look. "You didn't know? Really?"

Hank shook his head. "I don't keep up with the alumni page much, I'm afraid." A large hand clamped down on his shoulder and Hank was whirled around to face an obsessively broad-shouldered man in a sharp-looking Armani suit.

"Then you wouldn't know we just got married." The bald man wore sunglasses and his grin showed one gold tooth, completing the overall look of a mob boss.

Hank felt his lungs collapse in the man's vice-grip embrace. Released, Hank stood back and caught his breath. But when the man tore off his glasses, Hank's heart stopped. Could this day get any stranger? "Jake Clausen?" He looked from Cynthia to Jake. "You two"—he pointed from one to the other—"are married?"

The burly man, twice Hank's size, had once

been the star left tackle on the Northwestern offensive line. He was a moose then—an angry moose, as Hank recalled.

Jake picked up his wife's hand and kissed it tenderly. "Just a little over a month ago. Am I a lucky man, or what?" He smiled. Then, as though realizing they weren't alone, he turned to Hank and tugged on his suit. "Still getting used to the business attire." He chuckled.

"You look magnificent, baby," Cynthia cooed.

Oh, boy.

Hank wondered how much Jake knew about what his wife was like back in school, or about her penchant for football players—in particular the idiot sophomore who had climbed into her bedroom window on a dare from his pyromaniac friend, Pete.

He and Pete were lab partners and hence Pete had heard Hank's whining about his obsession with the young woman. He'd bet him he couldn't ask her out. Hank took the bet, but the dare was to be on Pete's terms. The Simmons's home, a late-century Victorian that looked more like a gothic castle than a residence, stood within an imposing black wrought-iron fence at the edge of the campus. Surrounded by ancient oak and pine, it was a virtual fortress, housing the dean's only daughter. A senior, she was the model of good genes, stellar upbringing, and impeccable taste—all of which appealed to the then sophomore. Asking her out—rather, how it was to be conducted—was a matter to which Hank had given great thought, in particular how to explain to his parents why he was expelled from school, if caught.

But…if she said yes, then he would be the man on campus, the envy of every starry-eyed male who pined after Cynthia. And his friend Pete, poor sap, would be one-hundred-bucks poorer. All he needed was tenacity, charm, and his football jersey—how could she say no?

Climbing in the bedroom window of the family home after midnight seemed like a good idea at the time. Those squats in practice aided in hustling up that old oak with the agility of a chimp. He'd been grateful that no Doberman guard dogs had appeared, suggesting that the myth that old man Simmons kept no less than four patrolling the yard was completely false.

Grateful to find the lock unlatched, he slid open the window, needing only a gentle nudge midway. He climbed in and promptly fell over something large and tufted, which he would later come to use to his advantage later. But now it alerted her pint-sized guard Maltese to start yapping and tearing at the pantleg of his football sweatpants. "Hey, these aren't cheap, Fido," Hank had whispered, trying to shake the mutt from his pantleg.

"Beastly, sit."

Hank looked up in surprise—more so that the dog had promptly plopped on his little butt than at seeing Cynthia sitting upright in bed in the soft glow of the bedside lamp.

"Are you the prince come to rescue this damsel in distress?" She smiled and twirled a strand of her hair as she assessed him sprawled across a pink-

WORTH THE WAIT

tufted ottoman. He was about to answer when a short round of raps sounded on her bedroom door.

"Cynthia, what is going on in there?"

Hank scrambled to his feet and ducked his head to climb back out on the roof.

Apparently finding the whole thing hilarious, she'd ordered him under the bed, scooped up the dog, and proceeded to concoct a story about how she'd tripped when she got up and forgot to turn on the light.

Hank had held his breath. With little else to do but wait, he couldn't help but notice the contrast of cleanliness between the underside of her bed to his. But his discoveries didn't stop there. He picked up an object he'd only heard about, never held, something girls had often referred to as their "little electric boyfriend."

The door closed. Crawling out from his hiding place, he handed her the curious toy, asking how it worked. Cindy turned out the light and switched herself *on*.

For the next three weeks, they engaged in a purely physical relationship, making out whenever they could, whenever they could. It was the first time he'd given a football shirt to a woman. He prayed she'd gotten rid of it. It all ended when the new redshirt walk-on took over as quarterback mid-season.

"You know what? We should have dinner tonight." Cynthia smiled, putting her hands together with a joyful look. "I know Daddy would love to see another one of Northwestern's best players."

Yep. The day had just gotten stranger.

Daddy? "Your father...is here?" A bead of sweat popped up and trickled down the length of Hank's spine. Maybe it was just the heat of the day. Either way, he'd spent too much time avoiding direct contact with the man while in college. He wasn't about to tempt fate now.

"He flew in to meet his friends from Chicago and play golf."

"He came to play golf with Alistair Rhoades?" Hank asked.

"Yeah, they've been friends for years. Mother was glad to get rid of him for a few days. He gets antsy when he sits around too much." She smiled at her husband then, giving his chin a playful tweak. "Jake here has promised to take him to the gun range this afternoon, maybe you'd like to join them?"

Hank was fairly certain this range had nothing to do with roaming buffalo.

"Jake's quite the marksman as well as football player."

"Wow, that's...just great." Hank's phone vibrated on the table. He picked it up and saw it was Julie. Thanking the good lord above, he looked at the couple. "I'm sorry. I've got to take this. Excuse me."

He walked inside the vestibule to the bar—*sans* a bartender as it was too early—and watched as a waiter readied the tables for the lunch crowd. Looking at the photo on his phone, he saw how happy they were the night they'd taken the selfie at the Café Du Monde. Maybe she'd finally found a moment to explain why she'd given a stranger permission to stay in his cabin.

"Hey, sweetheart. How are you?" He climbed onto a bar stool and leaned his elbow on the polished mahogany countertop.

"Have you seen the news?" she asked.

It took him a moment to realize her voice teetered on the verge of panic. He glanced up at the dark screen of the television hanging in the corner over the bar. "Hey, can I get this turned on, please?" he called to the waiter.

"I've got it, Jessie." Cynthia passed behind him and rounded the end of the counter. She pointed the remote at the wide screen TV.

"Is there a news station?" he prompted Cynthia.

Jake walked in and stood beside him.

"We're looking for a news station," Hank told Julie. "Are you okay? Are the boys okay?"

"I hope so. I just saw the news about a wildfire that started earlier southwest of Denver," Julie said. "I wasn't sure if I should—"

"Wait, this is good. Could you please turn it up?" Hank kept one eye on the screen. "I'm seeing the report now, honey." A map of the area appeared on screen.

"Officials aren't saying as yet what they feel started the fire. With no storms or lightning in the area, it's suspected to be accidental—or maybe arson. And the drought that's been plaguing this area the past few weeks is not helping firefighters," the newscaster said.

Hank focused again on Julie. "Have you heard from Kyle?"

"Not a word since he left," she said.

Hank held back a frustrated sigh. "The camp is miles from where the fires are," he assured her. "You can bet those leaders are keeping a close eye on things."

"I've tried calling," Julie said. "I remember reading that the boys' cell phones might be out of range once they get up there in the mountains."

"Just stay close to the phone," Hank said. "They're Scouts. Always prepared, right?"

"I suppose. I'd feel better if I could hear from him that he's okay," she said.

"There's a good chance he'll call if he can get a signal. He's trying to be like the other guys."

"You mean, who also aren't calling their parents?"

"They're kind of at that age, Jules. No longer a child, not quite a man."

"Maybe you could try?"

"Oh, I'd already planned on it, honey," Hank replied. "And I'll let you know the minute I hear anything."

"Thank you, Hank," she said, her voice softer now.

"Hang in there. It's going to be fine." He waited a heartbeat, hoping she'd mention the guy living next door…in his cabin.

She released a deep breath. "Okay," she said. "I need to run. Chris and I have an appointment."

"Okay." No mention of the stranger. The connection ended.

"Is there anything we can do to help?" Cynthia asked.

Hank sat for a moment, trying to stay calm,

WORTH THE WAIT

rational—just as he'd suggested to Julie. He looked from one to the other. "I may need to leave early. My fiancée's son is at a Scout camp near Denver and, understandably given the wildfires, she's concerned." He had a sudden thought. "Pete," he said, not realizing he'd done so aloud.

Jake frowned. "Who's Pete?"

"Pete Taylor," Hank said. "You remember him from chem lab?"

Jake thought for a moment, then snapped his fingers. "You mean that guy who used to get caught like every other month setting off rockets in the middle of campus?" He shook his head. "The guy was a bona fide pyromaniac."

"Yeah, that guy took his skills and runs the smokejumpers training camp near Denver. We trained there the summer after I graduated. I didn't stay in, but Pete went on to make a career out of fighting fires. If anyone knows what's going on, it's him." Hank stood and tucked his phone in his pocket. "I'll give him a call, then fly home and talk to Julie."

"We'll take care of things here." Cynthia patted his shoulder. "You go do what you have to do and I hope everything is okay."

Jake slapped him on the back. "Wildcats forever, man. Anything you ever need, just call," he said.

She was trying to keep it together, struggling to trust in what Hank had said. No news is good news, she'd told herself. They are smart enough, if necessary, to evacuate those kids and then notify their parents.

Julie had turned her phone to vibrate so as not to interrupt Chris's session with Reverend Cook.

"You know, Chris, life is all about choices," Reverend Cook said. "Circumstances, our experiences, all can determine our choices—whether that's for the good or bad."

She heard her young son's audible sigh. He'd been dealing with anger issues stemming from the verbal abuse he'd received from his father, and exacerbated by the violent domestic standoff when his father had held them hostage.

Julie had only recently convinced him to visit with the reverend about his experience. Julie hadn't been to church in years, But Reverend Leslie Cook, pastor at the First Church of Christ in End of the Line, was no ordinary minister. She'd served a short time as chaplain in the military and had traveled to a number of VA hospitals across the Midwest before accepting the position at the church. Raised by her divorced, single mom, she'd watched her mother battle depression, and she understood teenage anger. Glad that Clay had suggested her, Julie formed an immediate bond with the woman, who'd told her that she believed Providence had brought her to End of the Line. It was clear Reverend Cook knew a thing or two about making choices.

Julie fought not to check her phone as she waited for Hank to call. It was the reverend's only request…that she shut off all cell phones during sessions.

"I believe we're given a free will. All of us—me, your mom, and you. Now, with that comes a lot of responsibility, because our choices can also create consequences."

Chris's expression remained solemn. He sat slumped in his seat, occasionally tapping his fingers on the chair arm. He'd been silent thus far, but he straightened now and cleared his throat. "What I hear you saying is if I hate my dad, it's not a good thing—not the Christian thing to do, right?" Chris asked.

Reverend Cook regarded the boy, darting a quick glance at Julie before she spoke. "You know, Chris, I'm not here to tell you how you should live your life—how you should feel or whether that makes you a good Christian or not. Being a good person has nothing to do with being a Christian—it's a reflection of the spirit within us. In and of ourselves, not a one of us is perfect, or without sin, for that matter."

Chris snorted.

"But here's the thing," the pastor continued. "You don't have to agree with what someone does, or how *they* act. It's really about how you react that matters."

Chris looked puzzled.

"Let me explain. Those things you hate most, that are making you so angry, are robbing you of seeing and enjoying the good things—the blessings, if you will—in your life. Do you understand what I'm saying?" she asked.

Chris chewed on his lip as though thinking things through. "I think so."

Julie's heart twisted. The reverend's words hit close to home. Being with Hank, enjoying his company, was safe. It made her happy. But it was easier to keep him at arm's length, protecting her heart from being hurt again. Fear had kept her from seeing some of the real blessings she had right in front of her.

She stood and took the seat next to her son. "May I say something?"

Reverend Cook nodded, her smile kind.

Julie turned to her son. "I've just this moment realized how much I've been allowing my fears to keep me from seeing what's good in my life." She looked closely at her son, realizing he stood on the brink of becoming a teen, an age in which kids rely on stability as much as they rebel against it. She searched his eyes—eyes that had seen the worst, experienced a betrayal of trust from someone he should've been able to count on. "Neither you, Kyle, nor me are to blame for your father's choices." She covered his hand with hers. "Nor do we have to live our lives as victims of his choices."

Chris seemed to study her. She saw the moment wisdom and understanding flickered across his features. "Does that mean you're finally going to marry Hank?"

Julie's breath caught. She looked at the pastor, who cocked her head as though to challenge her response.

Julie looked at her son. "I suppose I've been afraid to commit."

"Ya think, Mom?" Kyle said. "Just so you know, because you've never asked—I think Hank is pretty cool. We really like him. And to be honest, Mom, Kyle and I don't understand why you keep putting off getting married. It would be great to be a family."

A light switched on in Julie's head. "Has that

made you angry?" she asked.

Chris shrugged. "Not so much angry, just really confused. I mean, come on, Mom, we know where he sleeps when he's at the ranch."

Julie glanced at the pastor and felt her cheeks warm.

Reverend Cook held up her palms. "Not judging."

"Hank is a really good guy. We think he'd make a great dad. I don't get that, if we see it, why don't you?"

Maybe it had taken a child to lead her to the truth. "I'm not really sure I ever thought about when or if I might marry."

"Chris," the reverend said, "there's a small fridge with sodas just outside my office. Why don't you grab one and give your mom and I a moment?"

"To talk, right?" He stood and started towards the door, but made a quick U-turn and hugged his mom around the shoulders before he left.

Julie sat in stunned silence, grappling with this revelation. All this time, she'd assumed her son's frustration was directed solely towards his father. It never occurred to her that her behavior might also play a role.

"So, how'd you feel about that?" Reverend Cook asked.

Julie let the information sink in. Certainly, they'd all needed time to get past the initial trauma of what had happened to them, but her boys had been watching, perhaps more carefully than she thought, how she treated Hank. Had she been leading him on until something better came along? It appalled her to think she was capable of such a thing. "My first thought is how blind I've been." Julie met the pastor's gaze.

"Give yourself a little grace, Julie," Reverend Cook said. "You've had a lot to deal with. Sometimes fear lies to us, telling us we're protecting ourselves or others when really it's keeping us from accepting the gifts placed in front of us."

"I feel like I've been so unfair to Hank," Julie said.

"Well, I'm not advocating that you jump into marriage, certainly not out of guilt or obligation." She leaned forward, folding her arms on the desk. "Or if you truly have concerns." She lifted a brow. "But, if you love the man, if he's good to your kids and they like him, if he wants to partner with you to offer a stable family life, then I'd have to ask…what are you waiting for? What are you afraid of here, Julie?"

"Being hurt?" Julie said, realizing that her fear was unfounded. Hank was a good man, an excellent lover, a good friend, and he'd make a great dad to her boys—all-in-all a wonderful life partner.

Reverend Cook smiled. "I can't guarantee that any relationship won't result in one or both parties getting their feelings hurt once in a while. I think the key here is whether you feel Hank is the kind of person that you can talk it through and be okay with at the other end." She shrugged. "Hank has always impressed me as being a reliable, grounded guy. I suspect that's part of why you fell for him. Am I right?"

Julie's chin quivered, a lump rising in her throat. Tears stung the corners of her eyes. "Yeah, I never

WORTH THE WAIT

stopped to think about it." She nodded. "And for so many other reasons that I'm just waking up to."

Reverend Cook sat back and smiled at her. "You know, my calendar is pretty clear the next couple of months. Nobody has scheduled any weddings around here." She flipped through her desk day-planner and glanced at Julie.

With much on her mind, and still no word from Hank, Julie did a quick scan of her checklist as she waited for all of her committee chairs to arrive at the diner, quiet now that the lunch crowd had parted.

Betty had just placed on the table a plate of fresh cookies sent over from Rebecca at the bakery and a tray with hot coffee and mugs. She settled in a chair and pulled a pencil from her blond beehive hairdo and looked at Julie, poised to take notes.

Coach Justin Reed slid into a chair and immediately reached for a mug and a couple of cookies. "I didn't get lunch today. Planned to order something after the meeting. I say eat dessert first." He smiled and wolfed down one and then another of the warm chocolate chip cookies.

Sally hurried in, placed her notebook on the table. "Hey, I'm here, it's just that...well, you'll have to excuse me a moment. Be right back." She hurried around the corner without further explanation.

Julie met Betty's curious gaze as she poured Julie a cup of coffee and handed it to her. "Nan and Wyatt are the only ones left."

Julie hadn't seen or spoken to Nan in a couple of

days, not since they'd discovered the unexpected letter amongst her husband's military possessions.

Julie waited a few moments, hoping Nan would show. She'd decided that, if necessary, she would take over the veterans' float responsibilities. "I guess we'll go ahead, then," Julie said, starting the meeting. She'd promised her son pizza and a movie tonight and she aimed to keep her promise. "Coach Reed? How are the plans coming for the rodeo?"

Justin Reed, a transplant along with his wife and son from Atlanta, now ran a horse ranch just north of town. He was also the head coach of the Varsity football team at End of the Line High school. Justin checked his notebook, his preferred form of checklist as opposed to a smartphone app. "Wednesday night after the parade, we've got mutton busting and a junior rodeo lined up for the younger kids. Nothing dangerous." He glanced at Julie. "Your brother mentioned your concerns. I promise, they'll be well padded and wear helmets."

"Thank you," Julie said, making note to smack Clay upside the head next time she saw him.

"Thursday will be the crowning of the rodeo king and queen, followed by the tractor pull event and the best cattle dog show." He flipped a page and continued. "Friday, I've lined up a local band and Dusty has agreed to put up a beer tent, providing we can get the proper permits from the city council…might have a guy who can wrangle up some nice fireworks for one of the nights."

Julie was impressed at the amount of organization that he'd done. "With all you've planned for

WORTH THE WAIT

the weekdays, how on earth do you plan to top that on Saturday?"

Justin grinned. "We'll have the cook-off that morning, while the farmers market and artists are downtown. In the afternoon we're going to have some friendly barrel racing by some of the best on the circuit. And following that, an amateur bronc riding contest. One-hundred-dollars entry fee, per contestant, with the purse going to a local charity. I thought we could bounce around a few ideas for a worthy recipient."

Betty applauded. "Well done, Coach. You're quite good at this."

Justin offered a sheepish look and grinned. "I can't take all the credit. Georgia has some heavy-duty connections through some of the people she met at the bar we have down in Atlanta. She's been bustin' my chops to stay on top of this."

"I knew I liked that girl." Betty smiled. She looked at Julie.

"Nan's next, but we could skip over her and go to you, Betty, since Nan's not here yet."

"She's just running a bit late," Betty said. "She'll be along any minute."

Julie wasn't entirely convinced. She made a mental note to go check on her after the meeting. "Please, go ahead, Betty."

"Well," Betty began with a pleased smile, "we've gotten over fifteen local entries and at least three from Billings. We're charging a twenty-five-dollar entry fee and I wanted to see what you all thought of selling off servings of the entries with all proceeds going to the county food pantry."

"That's a wonderful idea," Julie said, making a

note on her list.

"Jerry and I have talked about this and we'd like to offer breakfast every morning of the festival. You know, a variety of breakfast sandwiches, burritos, hash browns, and juice and coffee, of course. We'd like to donate proceeds from that to Miss Ellie's shelter down in Billings."

Sally clasped her hands together and smiled. "Betty, that is amazing. Ellie will be thrilled."

"That woman has done so much for us here in this community. It seems only right we do the same for her," Betty said.

Julie had heard about Miss Ellie, but hadn't had the chance to get to know her well. But her reputation was well-known among many in End of the Line. She'd been integral in helping Angelique out of a dangerously abusive relationship. Angelique's story was tumultuous. Nearly killed by her ex, she'd survived and found happiness with Dalton Kinnison, her first love, along with their daughter, Emilee.

Ellie had also been crucial in securing a permanent home for Cody, a young boy whose drug-addicted mother's life was tragically ended in a deal gone bad.

Rein and Liberty had fostered the child, applied for his adoption, and, soon after, the three became a family.

"That sounds wonderful, Betty." Julie read over her notes for the veterans' float and again tried to quell her concern for Nan.

"Sorry I'm late. I had breakfast with Gwen," Nan said, scooting into the empty chair between Justin and Sally.

CHAPTER SIX

Hank had waited through three rings, his phone propped under his chin as he multi-tasked, packing his bags. He was about to hang up when a woman came on the line.

"Denver Smokejumper Training Camp. Mr. Taylor's office," she said.

"I'd like to speak with Pete Taylor, please," Hank said, taking hold of the phone. They hadn't spoken in some time. After graduation, Pete had talked Hank into going out to Colorado and training as a wildland firefighter. Both had possessed the physical requirements and, despite being called every synonym for "lunatic" by friends and family members, both had persevered. There, Hank had discovered his love for planes and had considered pursuing a career flying the big airtankers or carrying smokejumpers into places where the firefighters couldn't go.

"May I ask who's calling?" the receptionist said.

"Hank Richardson."

"One moment, please."

His father had been livid. His mother couldn't understand why her only son would choose such a life-threatening profession, given they'd both expected him to take his place in the vice-president's office across the hall at his father's business.

"They pay people to risk life and limb like that?" his mother had asked. "You couldn't pay me enough to leap into a forest fire."

"It's not about the money, Mom. It's about making a difference, helping people."

"Your father has had a lifetime of helping people in his line of work, Henry," she reminded him.

"In a different way, true. This is about saving lives. Being a first responder," he said. Certain that, with time, they would come to accept his choices, he continued, passing the National Wildfire Basic Training course and receiving his red card.

But life changed in the blink of an eye.

Just after Hank passed the course, his father suffered a severe heart attack, effectively changing the trajectory of Hank's future. His mother had called, frantically begging him to come home. She needed him to take over the reins to the business while his father recuperated. Being the firstborn and heir to the men's clothing empire his father had created loomed before him. And though it apparently wasn't in his future to become a hot-shot smokejumper, nor was it his desire—much to his parent's dismay—to step in and run the corporate side of the family business.

So, he'd relinquished the responsibility to his sister, Caroline. She was far better suited to the corporate lifestyle, and in need of purpose after a recent break-up with her wealthy European boyfriend.

Back home, Hank had worked to gain his commercial pilot's license. He then bought a plane and

WORTH THE WAIT

started a private charter service. It had not taken his father long to forgive him, once he realized the convenience a private plane afforded his company.

A deep-throated cough brought Hank from his reverie.

"Man alive. Hank Richardson, you old dog. What's shakin', trouble?" Pete asked in his bright, devil-may-care voice.

Hank smiled. He'd not heard his old nickname in years. Of course, it had been given to him in the years he'd spent in the company of Pete, Clay, and the Kinnsion boys. "Hey, man. How's it going? You still able to still keep up with those young guys?" Hank asked.

Pete chuckled, his voice lower, grittier than Hank remembered. "They like to think they're hot shit on a cracker. Some of them have balls of steel." He laughed. "Reminds me of us back in the day…fearless, cocky, invincible." He paused. "Say, you aren't thinking of giving up running rich people hither and yon and getting your butt out here to help me out? We sure could use a guy with your mad flying skills. Seems like the recruits are dwindling each year. The military offers better benefits after college."

"Yeah, but you wouldn't be anywhere else, am I right?" Hank said, zipping his duffel shut.

"Call me looney. I still love it," Pete said with a laugh that quickly descended into a coughing fit.

Hank frowned. It was no surprise that years of being around fire and smoke would affect one's health, but this was his crazy, reckless friend Pete. It was difficult not to see him as immune to occupational hazards. "You okay?"

"Sure, sure," Pete responded. "To what do I owe the pleasure of this call? Catching up? Need an application form?"

"I was hoping you might have some information," Hank said.

"Shoot, I'll do what I can." Pete held the phone away from his mouth and coughed again.

"I was wondering if you had any information on the fires out west? My fiancée's kid is at a Scout adventure camp northwest of Denver," Hank said. "It's his first time."

"And hers, it sounds like." Pete said. "We've been receiving updates all morning. Let me see what's come in."

Hank heard the tapping of a keyboard.

"Whereabouts is the camp?"

"Near Gypsum."

"Uh-huh." More typing followed.

"Yeah, Julie had tried calling, but couldn't get through," Hank said.

"That's pretty normal in that area." Pete paused. "Julie? No chance in hell that's the same Julie you fell head over heels for after your junior year?"

Hank chuckled. "One and the same." He slung his bag over his shoulder, scanned the room once more, and headed to the elevator.

"Damn, you know how to pick 'em, son. Course, I never thought there'd be anyone after the dean's daughter. What was her name again?"

"Cynthia," Hank said. "She married that monster of a left tackle, Jake Clausen."

"No shit? And you two are still in touch? I have to say, I'm a little jealous." Pete laughed.

"Not exactly. I hadn't spoken to her since we broke up. As it turns out, she and Jake own the resort I flew my clients to here in southern California. Her dad had just flown in to meet those same guys."

"Whoa. You saw old man Simmons? How'd that go?" Pete asked, his enthusiasm animated.

"Fortunately, he was out playing golf. I'm on my way to the airport now to fly back to make sure Julie and Chris are okay. Thought I'd grab my gear and head down to Denver to see if I can pick up Kyle a little early. Just to be safe. Think his mom would feel a lot better."

"Understand that," Pete said. "Checking the radar map, it looks like the camp is well southeast of the fires. They're working aggressively on the ridge a couple of hundred miles away. Thus far we've been placed on alert, but haven't received any orders yet."

"So, you'd assume that officials would probably at least apprise campers and the Scout camp of the situation, right?" Hank asked.

"DNR should be on top of notifying the public," Pete said. "I have a buddy over at the western Utah base. Let me give him a call. See what he knows."

"That'd be great, Pete. If its not too much trouble. I imagine that Julie's not the only concerned parent out there."

"Absolutely. Hey, I'll call you back."

"Thanks, man. Who knows, she may have heard something by the time I get home," Hank said.

"You know, we're going to have to get together and catch up," Pete said. "You know I've been offered a position as head trainer at the Montana smokejumper base. I could use the help."

Hank felt an old spark ignite his passion, but he'd set it aside a long time ago. Besides, he had Julie and the boys to think about now. "Congratulations, Pete, and thank you, I'm honored you asked. While it's tempting, I'm not sure that it's a good time to entertain the idea, what with a new fiancée and two sons in the package deal," Hank said. "But you'll have to come down when you get settled. End of the Line is not far down the road. The Kinnisons run an equine rescue ranch. Rein and his wife run cabin rentals on the ranch, and you remember Clay, Julie's brother? He moved there a couple of years ago and is married with twin girls now."

"Dayum," Pete said. "I can't even find a date on our website smokinghot.com. Sounds like I need to visit End of the Line."

"Hey, you never know," Hank said. "Betty, she owns the diner—amazing food, by the way—says that folks come to End of the Line to begin again. She may be right about that."

"Then I'll mark my calendar," Pete said with a chuckle.

"I'm headed to the airport," Hank said. "Let me know what you find out."

Julie's eyes met Nan's, her admiration for the woman rising off the charts. She wasn't at all certain she would be able to handle the situation Nan found herself in with such grace.

"How is Gwen these days?" Betty asked. "I'm

WORTH THE WAIT

so glad her kids decided to bring her home." She shook her head, her eyes filled with sympathy.

Julie glanced at Nan. In her short time in End of the Line, Julie had discovered that most people in this town were very caring and ready to help anyone in need. She and her boys had been direct recipients, from the Kinnisons giving her a cabin to live in to Betty offering her a job when she wasn't sure how to put her own life back together. Trusting others again hadn't been easy for Julie, and in some ways, she was still learning. Yet another reason she wasn't ready to set a date.

Nan was contemplative before she spoke. "She has good and bad days, but I'm afraid she hasn't recognized me since I've been visiting her."

Julie did understand the ravages of the disease, having watched painfully as it had nibbled away at her mother. They'd placed her in an assisted living facility while Clay was overseas. By the time he returned, she didn't recognize him at all. It had been difficult for Clay, having lost all of his team in a roadside bomb. He was the lone survivor and the loss of his leg sent him home only to find that his fiancée wasn't able to handle his physical and emotional state. Clay had fallen into a state of deep despondency, and that's when Julie had called Dalton for help.

"Are you okay?" Julie asked. To those at the table, it implied that she asked because Gwen was an old friend. But her concern ran deeper, and Nan knew it.

"I'm fine," she bristled. "If you don't mind, I'd like to give my report. Have a ton of things to do today." Her gruff attitude was part of her personality. Everyone accepted it. She'd had to run the store and repair shop alone for several years, occasionally hiring high school kids for extra help. To look at her, most saw a weathered, frail-looking woman, but Nan could fix a tractor as good as any man in town and wasn't afraid to say so.

Julie listened as Nan outlined in detail the men and women she'd lined up to ride on the veterans' float.

"Of course, it depends on the health of some whether they'll be well enough to ride. But Wyatt was going to help me take a look at the flatbed and see if we could rig up spots for a few wheelchairs." She frowned. "And he was going to take a look at that axle, too. We need to get that fixed," she said to herself.

"Good morning."

Everyone looked up to find Hunter standing in the small entryway into the room used for private parties.

"I hope it's okay if I step in for Wyatt this morning. Aimee was feeling a little under the weather. He asked if I'd mind just sitting in and let Nan—" He looked around the table, his gaze landing on the woman in question. "You must be Nan." He held his large hand out, swallowing hers. "I think you're the only one here I haven't met." He offered a charming smile.

Julie was as equally charmed as her female friends, watching the introduction play out—and that included Nan. Julie noticed a bit of pink tinged the woman's weathered cheeks.

"I understand you're holding my truck hostage in your garage?"

That brought a wider smile from Nan. "So, that's your truck Dalton hauled in. Vintage model, that one. But hard as hell to find parts for."

"Yeah, it was my dad's." He lay his other hand atop hers, holding it a moment more. "I really appreciate whatever you can do, ma'am."

"You know anything about axles?" Nan asked.

"Raised on a farm in Texas," Hunter said with a smile. "I tinkered around a bit."

"Good." Nan stood and gathered her things. "Let's walk over to the garage and see if you can tinker with that axle on the flatbed we need for the parade. I can show you what I've ordered for your truck, but I have to be honest, these folks aren't the fastest people on the face of the earth."

Hunter stepped aside and waited as Nan slung her canvas bag over her arm.

"May I carry that for you?" he asked.

Nan raised a brow and handed him the bag.

Julie opened her mouth to tell Nan that she'd stop by later, but Nan had taken Hunter's proffered arm and was chatting as the two walked away from the table.

"That boy could charm the skin off a snake," Betty said with a chuckle.

"He's adorable," Sally said. "Did you hear that drawl when he said ma'am?"

"He's just being a true southern gentleman, ladies," Justin chimed in, letting go his Georgia drawl.

Julie rolled her eyes. Not that she wasn't just as smitten by how the man had treated her friend. After all, Nan could use a little southern-gentleman-style care in her life right now. She had found it interesting however, how easily Nan had taken to Hunter. It wasn't like her to be quite so trusting with strangers. She shook the thought from her head, having much more on her plate at the moment.

"Sally? How's the community choir tribute coming?"

Sally was End of the Line's one and only music teacher, in addition to being Julie's beautiful sister-in-law and mother to the most adorable twin girls in the known world. Seeing how life here in End of the Line had changed her brother for the better had been key in Julie's decision to move there and offer her two boys a new start. Sally's passion for music was exceeded only in the love she showed for Clay and those two girls. "We've had a couple of rehearsals of the church choirs. Reverend Cook and Reverend Bishop have kindly each offered their churches for the performance. We're currently in the throes of deciding which one to use."

Betty grinned. "You know, I can't help but think that those two would be a force to be reckoned with if they ever got together."

Sally's eyes opened wide. "You don't think that's why they aren't making a decision, just so they can spend time together?"

Betty shrugged. "Stranger things have happened around here." She cast her gaze to the ceiling. "I swear I could write a book."

Julie checked off the last item on her to-do list and sighed. "Church choice notwithstanding"—she glanced at Betty—"or potential book deals, I have to say thank you for how on top of things you all are. I'll be talking to Charlene at the courthouse today to see how the paperwork is coming on the permits we'll need. And to see that the dedication of the railroad depot is ready to go on time. Rein and Liberty have been working hard to restore it to its original state."

Betty nodded. "They nearly gutted the inside from back in the sixties when they converted the depot to a bus station. When the bus stopped coming here, the old place sat empty. I can remember that was the mode of transportation for lots of folks back then."

"I'm just glad to see we're trying to get it certified on the registry of historic places. Boy, if those walls could talk," Sally said.

"Indeed," Justin said. "It was started as a railroad depot back when they'd just discovered gold in the mountains. Unfortunately, there wasn't as much as they thought, but by then a lot of men had brought their wives and families here to settle down. Many, who'd already been traveling place to place looking for their gold stake, decided to stay and became ranchers and farmers, instead." He smiled. "It's rumored that's why the founding fathers called it End of the Line."

"You've done your research, Coach," Betty grinned.

"Teaching history is my first passion," Justin said. "I was talking to Rein the other day and he mentioned that, in his Uncle Jed's diary, they discovered that the Kinnisons go way back to the formation of this town."

"That's right," Sally said. "I remember Aimee telling me that's how they came up with Christian Ezekiel's name." She smiled. "The more I learn about this town, the prouder I am to live here. We have a lot to celebrate."

A squeal of toddler laughter erupted from the doorway. Aubrey and Ava Marie Sanders sat side-by-side in a double-stroller being pushed by their father, Clay.

"Meeting adjourned," Julie said. "I'll email the date of the next meeting. You all are the best." Julie followed the group out into the main dining area. A few patrons had come in for a quick cup of coffee or a fresh slice of one of Rebecca's pies, well aware of the scheduled time when they came out of the bakery oven and appeared on the diner's shelf.

Julie reached down to unbuckle one of her nieces. She snuggled the little girl, oblivious to her sticky fingers from eating her little cereal snacks.

"Hey, Jules. How's it going?" Clay pulled out a chair and guided the stroller alongside so he could manage the girls. Sally had excused herself to go to the restroom—something, Julie had noticed, she'd done at least twice during the meeting. "You guys have any particular news you're keeping under wraps?" She leaned close to her brother with a grin.

Clay returned a blank look. Either he was very good at bluffing or totally clueless. Julie was banking on the latter. "Going for number three?" she asked, more to the point.

He looked perplexed for a moment, then glanced over his shoulder to where his wife had gone. "We've been trying to keep it quiet," he said as he pushed closer to Julie.

"I think you might have been successful," Betty

said, lowering her voice as she ducked her head into the private conversation.

Apparently, she, too, had noticed Sally's frequent disappearances.

Betty patted Clay's shoulder. "Seen enough of the signs in my day," she said with a short laugh.

Clay sat back in his chair and shook his head. "Is nothing sacred in this small town?"

"No," both women stated in unison.

"Speaking of..." Clay offered his sister a pointed look. "I heard something about Hank taking more time on this trip. Trouble in paradise?"

Julie frowned. "No trouble at all," she said. "His clients offered him a bonus if he'd fly them to another resort. We decided it'd be that much more toward the wedding."

Clay looked elated. "Then you've set a date?"

She averted her gaze. "Not yet. Soon."

"How soon, Sis?"

Julie looked back at the concern on her brother's face. "I don't know...soon."

"Jules," Clay stated quietly, nodding his thanks to Betty for the coffee she placed in front of him. "You know Hank's a hot commodity."

"It's good to know that my brother thinks so." Julie smiled as she took a sip from Clay's cup.

"A *taken* commodity, to be certain," Betty offered, her advice unsolicited but always appreciated.

"Thank you, Betty," Julie said, acknowledging the woman's support. Everyone in town seemed to know that she'd been the one to delay the wedding plans. But when it came right down to it, the choice was theirs and theirs alone. *Yours, actually,* her conscious reminded her. "Could we discuss just about anything else?" she asked, offering her brother a congenial smile.

"Sure," he said. "How's the new neighbor?"

"Seriously?"

Clay shrugged. "Just asking. Dalton mentioned that Hank called him and wanted to know how you were doing."

"He's checking up on me?" She bristled at the idea that he didn't trust her. Then again, was she being trustworthy toward Hank?

"No, seems he was checking up on you after having a strange phone call with you the other night. Apparently, he felt a disconnect. Hank didn't even know about Hunter until Dalton mentioned him living at the cabins."

"Oh." Julie felt contrite, if not a tad guilty, for not having mentioned Hunter or the fact that she'd offered him the cabin next to hers while his truck was in repair.

"Yeah, he noticed you didn't mention him." Clay's brow knit as he held her gaze. "You getting cold feet, Jules?"

Was she? Why wouldn't she mention meeting Hunter if there was nothing to be concerned over? Then again, she justified mentally, they had others things to discuss. It wasn't important at the time. *Important enough that your palms were sweating as you spoke to Hank on the phone and it was only stray thoughts about the stranger making that happen.* "No." She straightened. "Just because I…we haven't set a date, just because I may find another man attractive…"

Clay tipped his head. Oh, yeah, he took notice

of that.

"It doesn't mean that I'm getting cold feet," she continued, or that I'm going to go out and make poor choices."

He held his hands up in defense. "Okay. Okay. I get it." He searched her eyes. "I'm here, though, if you need to talk."

Julie leaned forward and kissed his cheek. "Thanks, your concern is noted and appreciated, but entirely unnecessary."

Sally returned from the ladies' room looking a tad green around the gills. "Clay, do you mind if we go home? I don't think I'm up for pie today."

Julie buckled her niece into the stroller, kissing each cherub-faced girl on the cheek. She stood and gave Sally a hug. "Call if you need me to help watch the girls."

CHAPTER SEVEN

HANK SHOVED ASIDE THE THOUGHT that Julie hadn't mentioned loaning out his cabin to the new stranger in town.

"Everything looks good, Mr. Richardson," the airport mechanic, a man by the name of Ray Davidson told him. He'd known Ray for several years, meeting him first back in Chicago where he worked at Midway. "Would have had her ready," he said, wiping his hands on a grease rag. "I must have marked my calendar wrong. Swore you told me you'd fly out Thursday. Though I had a few days yet."

Hank shook the man's hand. A little dirt on his hands didn't bother Hank, but it would have repulsed his father. "No problem, Ray. I had a change in my schedule. Emergency back home." *My fiancée may be flirting with a handsome stranger*, he thought to himself, and then batted away the idea.

The mechanic frowned. "I hope everything's okay."

Hank nodded as he loaded his gear into the plane. "I'm sure it will be. Have a boy—well, my fiancée's boy—up at a camp in Colorado. They've got some wildfires in the White River Forest area that are a little too close for comfort. Thought I'd

WORTH THE WAIT

fly up there and get him. You know, in case."

Ray nodded. "I understand. My sister and her family live up in the mountains just west of Denver. I've been in contact with her, but she hasn't been notified of any evacuations yet. They say what started it?"

Hank slipped on his aviator glasses and climbed into the cockpit. "I haven't heard, but a friend of mine in Denver is checking into things. He said the authorities are pretty good at giving people ample time to evacuate."

Ray nodded, his lips flattened to a thin line as he frowned. "Just the same, I think I better give my sister a call." He closed the door behind Hank and offered a short wave as he walked across the tarmac.

Moments later, Hank's wheels left the McClellan Palomar runway en route to End of the Line. If all went as planned, it should be a little over two hours to touchdown.

According to his plan, that is.

Nothing since his disastrous attempt at a romantic proposal had gone according to plan. He tried to call Julie to let her know he was on his way to the ranch to pick up a few things from his training days in case he'd need them. The call rang several times before going to her voicemail.

"Hi, I'm unable to take your call, but leave a message and I'll get back to you as soon as I can. Have a great day."

"Hey, Jules," Hank said, searching the low-level clouds. "Letting you know that I'm on my way back home and, barring any weather, I should be arriving in a couple of hours." He paused, his thoughts taunting him with why she wasn't answering his call. Especially when he'd told her he'd keep her informed about what Pete found out. "Okay, hope you get this. See you soon. I love you." He laid the phone on the control panel.

His thoughts meandered back to his conversation earlier with Pete.

"You know, I've been offered a position as head trainer up at the Montana smokejumper camp. I could use a guy like you to help me."

Hank considered the future—at least, what seemed the foreseeable future. It was clear Julie seemed uncertain about setting a date, thought she had agreed to an engagement. Then there was the matter of whatever trust they had between them. Why hadn't she just told him about offering the cabin to the very handsome—according to Dalton—stranger? Why hadn't she assured him that he had nothing at all to worry about?

Rein had also known, and chances were good that the entire town knew about Mr. Wonderful occupying the cabin next to his fiancée. And, worse, he had to find it out from them instead of Julie.

Hank took off his glasses and rubbed his eyes. He'd thought that the proposal was going to be a step in the direction in setting down roots, being a real family, giving the boys and Julie a foundation—love, security. Instead, it seemed to create a chaotic domino effect on his life.

He picked up the phone, punched in the quick dial for Julie's number. It went straight to voicemail. He didn't leave a message, but disconnected with a number of thoughts, none of them good, racing through his mind.

"It's that white-knight syndrome," his sister's voice repeated in his brain.

Maybe she was right. A man secure in the knowledge of how his fiancée felt about him wouldn't be spinning his wheels about some guy needing a place to stay. After all, he was gone, the cabin was empty and all others full. Simple. Still, he couldn't help but reason, if Dalton picked up the guy, why didn't he offer him a room at his place?

He was for certain going to drive himself mad if he continued to dwell on this. He glanced at the phone and told himself to wait. "Crap," he said, and snatched up the phone. He punched her number again, and, as anticipated, got her voicemail. He waited impatiently through the message before leaving another of his own. "Hi, Jules. If you get this…I'm not exactly sure why you're not picking up, but give me a call." Hank paused. "Haven't heard from Pete. How's Chris? Okay, bye." He disconnected without any endearments, secretly hoping she might realize as much when she listened to the messages—*if* she listened to the messages.

He started to set the phone down when it rang. Hank answered, putting the phone to his ear without checking to see who it was. "Hello? Jules? I've been trying to call you for—"

"Hank, it's Pete," said the caller.

Hank mentally kicked himself. The stress was getting to him. He reeled in his emotions, teetering on edge. "Sorry, Pete. Thought you were someone else."

"I figured that. Listen, I can go if you're expecting a call, but I thought you'd want to know that I have an update on that fire."

"No, it's okay. What have you got?" Hank said.

"Sounds like a blast of southern air has turned the fire, fanning it northward in the Arapaho Forest."

"What does that mean?" Hank asked, unfamiliar with the territory. "Is that near the Scout camp?"

"Unfortunately, yes. We just got a call to move out. Evacuation protocol has begun at the National Park campgrounds and mountain residents in that area.

Hank checked his watch. "I'm about ninety minutes or so from the ranch. I'm going to refuel and then I'll head your way. What can I do to help?"

"What are you flying?" Pete asked.

"A Twin Otter," Hank answered.

"Excellent. Meet me at the Denver airport. Emergency helicopters and crew are meeting there to be briefed."

"Sounds good, Pete. And thank you."

"You bet," his friend said. There was a brief pause. "Not sure if you've ever thought about getting back into this, but I was very serious when I said I could use your help in this new position."

Hank kept his eyes on the horizon. A few days ago, when his immediate future involved setting a wedding date, Hank's answer might have been more decisive. If no plans were set by spring, maybe some time apart would help Julie realize what it was she wanted. Whether, in fact, she really loved him, or if she only felt some type of obligation for his involvement in rescuing her and the boys.

The very thought that her emotions might be so fickle sickened him. Could he have been so blind? Or had he only seen what he wanted to see? How much longer was he willing to wait? He had to consider his future. What might happen if this thing, God forbid, fizzled into nothing?

"You know, Pete, right now I just want to find Kyle and make sure he's safe." He hesitated, realizing this was a chance to fulfill a dream he'd set aside a long time ago. "Listen, though, I'm not adverse to talking more about this later. How's that?"

"Sounds great to me, man," Pete said. "We'll see you soon."

Hank hung up, looked at his phone, and debated whether to call Wyatt to see if Julie's car was in the drive. But with Julie giving the stranger his bed to sleep in, a phone call with his inquiry might start a whole landslide of rumors and speculation. Instead, he punched her quick dial and once more received her perky voicemail message. He disconnected, blowing out a frustrated sigh. He'd be home in a few minutes, anyway. Besides, there was probably a logical explanation for why she wasn't responding to his calls.

Probably.

Julie inhaled deeply. She loved driving the country road back to the ranch. With her windows rolled down, the scent of mown hay and pine warmed by the sun mingled into a heady fragrance at this time of year. A welcome northwest wind had blown in during the afternoon pushing everyone—animal and human—outdoors.

After the session earlier with Reverend Cook, Julie decided to take her advice and work on giving Chris consistency, establishing a routine so as to help him feel safe.

She slowed as she came down the small service road that trailed past the row of cabin rentals. With her windows rolled down, she swore she'd heard Chris's laughter—though he and Emilee were supposed to be helping muck stalls about this time of day while the horses were out to pasture.

She pulled into the short drive next to her cabin and looked up through her car window to see Hunter McCoy standing at the edge of their connecting backyards. He was dressed in camo shorts that exposed his muscular calves and a navy-colored T-shirt that was split on the sides, providing an eye-opening view of his ripped torso.

Julie stepped from the Jeep and shaded her eyes against the glint of the sun reflecting on the…was that a hatchet? Her eyes widened.

She left the groceries in the trunk and walked toward him, stumbling slightly as she navigated the small knoll between the two cabins.

"Let me show you guys one more time, then you can give it a try," Hunter said to an unseen guest.

Julie rounded the corner of the cabin and caught a glimpse of Emilee and Chris standing on the patio watching the man in rapt fascination.

A motion caught her eye and her gaze darted to Hunter. The hatchet left his grasp and spun end over end, landing with a resounding *thwack* against a crude handmade target made of barn-board propped against two bales of hay. A bullseye and rings had been sprayed on the wood, and a variety of hatchets and knives clung to the board.

Julie let out a yelp. What kind of barbaric game was this? She looked at Hunter. "What are you doing?"

Chris ran up to her, his eyes alive, an excited grin plastered on his face. "Hunter's teaching us how to throw hatchets. Isn't that cool?"

Julie scanned the faces of all three, who seemed to be wondering why she didn't share their enthusiasm.

"I hope you don't mind. I was telling them how my dad taught me this when I was their age," Hunter explained. With a confident swagger, even in flip-flops, he walked over and pulled the hatchets from the board.

Julie pointed to her son. "You—since I assume you've done your chores up at the barn—can take the groceries in and put them away."

"But Mom," he started with a high-pitched whine, only to have it crack midway.

"I should go. Grandfather will be wondering where I am," Emilee said. "Goodbye, Mr. McCoy. Mrs. Williams." She started around the house and stopped to pick up something in the grass. Studying it, she walked back to Julie, her steps slowing as she got closer. Her gaze came up, but it was not focused on Julie. She stared straight ahead. Julie had heard of the young girl's special abilities, though had not seen it in practice—if that's what this was.

Julie met her and held her hand out to accept the object. "Emilee, are you okay?" she asked.

The girl blinked and then nodded. She placed a pen knife in Julie's hand. "Grandmother said that I've been given a gift that helps people." She searched Julie's eyes.

"I'm sure that's true. Did you see something?" Julie asked.

Emilee nodded slowly. "Sometimes, if more than one person has owned an object, the pictures I see are hazy."

Julie recognized the pocketknife as the one Hank had given to Kyle on the day that he joined the Scouts. It had been given to Hank by his grandfather. "It must have fallen out of Kyle's pocket when he was mowing," she said.

"I couldn't see anything clearly. It was dark. That's all I can tell you," Emilee said. "I'm sorry."

"It's okay," Julie said, trying to shake off the strange, foreboding feeling in her gut. "You run on and find your grandfather."

The moment Emilee left, Julie pocketed the knife and turned to Hunter. "I'd like to know what you think you were doing? Teaching these kids about playing with bow knives and hatchets?"

"Well, I—"

"And without permission, I might add," Julie said. Her concern about Chris's safety muddied the situation. "Do you have any idea what might have happened?" She walked up toe-to-toe with him.

He held his ground, staring down at her. His all-male, musky scent teased her senses.

WORTH THE WAIT

He held her gaze. "I wouldn't let anything happen to either of those kids."

Julie's emotions went off the rail. Somewhere in her anger, she saw a pinpoint of logic in his words. Heck, hadn't she allowed her son to go off to tromp around the Colorado mountains, even given the multitude of unknown dangers? "Mr. McCoy, it is not your prerogative to decide what is best for my son, or for Emilee. I'm quite certain Dalton would have wanted to be asked first about this."

"It was his idea, actually." Hunter raked his thumbnail over his brow.

"Well, it wasn't mine and I'd appreciate you asking first before including my son in such activities. Do I make myself clear?" She sounded overprotective, she knew, but Chris was only just beginning to deal with his anger. Perhaps in time, hatchet-throwing might prove beneficial. Maybe even for her.

"Loud and clear, ma'am," he said with a brief salute.

Thankfully, Chris didn't bring up the hatchet topic as they ate their pizza and watched their favorite movie, *Goonies*. She'd not yet heard from Hank, but took comfort in the idea that no news was good news. She checked her hoodie pockets where she normally carried her phone and found them empty. Surprised, she uncurled from the couch and fished through her backpack. It wasn't there. She checked the kitchen, the bathroom, her bed, where she'd changed before making dinner.

The phone was nowhere to be found.

"What'd you lose?" Chris asked, glancing at her as he helped himself to another slice of pizza.

"Have you seen my phone?" she asked.

He shrugged and shook his head, already drawn back into the movie. She tapped her fingers on the kitchen counter, thinking back to the last time she had it out. Then she realized that she had it out when she'd been checking dates for the next meeting at the diner. She'd likely left it on the table, or on her desk in the back room when she went to shut down her computer. Hopefully, Betty had found it and put it in safekeeping until the morning. She'd check when she went in tomorrow. Meantime, she'd walk up to Wyatt and Aimee's and borrow their phone to give Hank a call.

"You stay put," she told her son. "I've got to run up to the main house and borrow a phone." She placed her hand on the doorknob and jumped when someone knocked loudly on the door.

Wondering who it could be at this hour of the night, she flipped on the light and peeked out the peephole. "Oh, brother," she muttered as she swung open the door.

Her handsome neighbor had changed into a full T-shirt and jeans, for which she should have been grateful. *Stop that.*

"I bring a peace offering," he said, holding up a stick in one hand and chocolate bars and a bag of marshmallows in the other. His long blond locks looked better than hers and she made a mental note to ask Lila, her hairdresser at the Curl Up and Dye salon, about a new conditioner.

"That's not necessary," she said, opening the

WORTH THE WAIT

door fully.

"I feel like maybe we've gotten off on the wrong foot," he said with a quick nod to the side. "I've got the firepit going out back and all the provisions." He offered a charming grin.

"Are we making s'mores?" Chris ducked under her arm and beamed up at Hunter. "I haven't had those in like forever, mom." He looked at her with pleading eyes.

Julie sighed. "Fine, but you still have to shower and get to bed early. You have to help Mr. Greyfeather—"

Her words were lost as her son rushed out and disappeared around the side of the house.

"Tomorrow," Julie finished. She glanced at her hunky neighbor. "I need to run up to the main house and borrow a cell phone."

"Mine's almost charged." He shrugged. "You're welcome to use it, unless it's an emergency and you need it right now."

She debated, figuring a few more minutes wouldn't matter and besides, if Hank had had an urgent message, he'd call Wyatt if he couldn't reach her. She grabbed her hoodie and followed him through the shadows between the cabins to where the fire glowed in the dark clearing.

Chris was already huddled near the fire, a marshmallow roasting over the flames.

Julie helped him assemble a s'more and sat back, gazing at the sprinkling of stars glittering in the night sky. The community style firepit, with its handmade Adirondack chairs built by Rein, were the perfect addition to the cabin rentals. Set a few yards from the back of the cabins in a clearing, it offered a full view of the sky.

Julie leaned her cheek on her hand and watched the joy on Chris's face. This was far more relaxing than she thought it would be. She glanced at Hunter seated across the fire from her. "I thought it was very nice how you and Nan seemed to get along right away."

He nodded. "She seems like a really nice lady. A very accomplished woman. Very independent."

"That she is, and doesn't take kindly to strangers so quickly." Julie smiled. She waded a little further into the waters of her curiosity. "I understand you're here to try to find your dad's birth mother?" She knew she was being nosy, perhaps only to quell her nerves with everything going on at present. But what were the odds that Hunter might have something to do with Nan's recent discovery?

"News travels fast," he said, eyeing the fire. "But, yes, I'm hoping to locate her, if possible. I'm not sure what I'll say if I do find her. I've not had grandparents before. My mom's parents passed on before I was born."

Julie nodded. Nan's secret was a tender subject. For now, perhaps it was best to let things play out. If an appropriate opening occurred later, she might say something to Nan. But she'd given the woman her word that she wouldn't discuss it with anyone else, and she would keep that confidence until Nan was ready to share it.

She glanced over and saw that gooey marshmallow covered more of Chris's fingers than what landed on his graham cracker.

"When you finish, young man, it's time for

your shower," she said pointing her thumb over her shoulder.

He scooped a glob of gooeyness from his chin and licked his fingers. "Do I have to?"

"Move it, mister." Julie stood. "I hope you find her," she said, watching Kyle run down the hill to their cabin. "Family is important."

"Oh, did you still need to use the phone?" Hunter asked.

Julie smacked her head. "Yes, thank you. I almost forgot." That, alone, should have sounded alarm bells in her head. How could she so quickly forget that she'd planned to call Hank?

"It's just inside." He stood and walked through the patio door ahead of her.

She stood in the dining room, admonishing herself mentally—in part because she'd lost her phone, and in part because she couldn't shake the sense that she felt awkward being alone with him and couldn't say why. He was probably used to women fawning over him, flirting with him. And that, she'd decide later, was what prompted her query. "Do you have someone special in your life?"

He glanced up and grinned. "Aren't you engaged?"

Julie caught the teasing tone of his comment.

"I wasn't asking for me, for goodness sake," she said, averting her eyes when he looked at her.

"Well, that's disappointing," he said with a chuckle. "Here I thought you were trying to seduce me."

Julie let out a short laugh. "I'm quite certain you have no trouble in that department."

He regarded her as though not quite sure of what she meant.

"I mean, you're not an ugly man, by any means," she said.

His expression was somewhere between confused and amused. "Thanks, I think." He held out the phone and she walked forward to take it from him. The toe of her shoe clipped the edge of the rug under the table and she pitched forward. Two muscular arms saved her from face-planting on the hardwood floor.

She was pulled upright, pressed against his chest. She caught her breath and brushed the hair back from her face. "Thank you," she said, looking up at him.

"It appears you get along well with the new neighbor."

Julie pushed from Hunter's grasp. Her gaze swerved to the front door where Hank stood, his keys still in the lock.

Hunter turned to face the door.

Julie felt the tension radiating off her fiancé. "Hank Richardson, this is Hunter McCoy. Hunter, this is Hank, my fiancé," she said in way of a quick and dirty introduction.

CHAPTER EIGHT

"MCCOY," HANK SAID, THEN GLANCED at Julie. "So, this is the guy sleeping in my bed." He pulled his keys from the door and pocketed them, then held out his hand to the strange man—who by God, *did* have a striking resemblance to Thor, for whatever that was worth. "See you've made yourself at home." He offered Julie a quick side-look. "We need to talk."

He walked between the two, probably on purpose. "I just need to get something from my closet," he said as he strode toward his bedroom. Or what used to be his bedroom. Hank shoved aside the poisonous thought of what he might have found had he arrived a few moments later.

"You didn't mention anything about coming home," Julie said from the doorway of the walk-in closet.

"That seems evident," he said quietly, digging through the few totes he'd brought from Chicago and stored here at the ranch. In truth, he'd begun a slow move to End of the Line with the assumption that he'd one day be here permanently.

He found the duffel bag in question and dragged it out into the room. He glanced at Julie as he hoisted the heavy bag onto the unmade bed. He didn't really care if a thousand closet spiders fell onto the sheets.

"I left my phone at the diner and just realized it," she said.

"That explains, then, why you haven't returned my calls."

"You could have called Wyatt if you couldn't reach me," she said. "He would have known to find me here…you know, at home."

"Yeah, I probably should have thought of that." He continued to yank items from the duffel, stuff he'd not seen since his days at wildfire training camp. His fireproof pants and jacket were still in good shape. His compass, helmet, and pickaxe all still looked remarkably good.

"I was just getting ready to call you." She punched his shoulder to gain his attention.

"I'm just going to step outside and give you two some privacy," Hunter said, appearing in the doorway.

"Fine," Julie responded in tandem with Hank.

Julie turned back to him. "What were you trying to call me about?" She planted her fists on her hips.

Any issues regarding their relationship, or what might be left of it, would have to wait. There were more pressing matters just now. "I left California to come check on you and Chris. I spoke to my buddy Pete, who said that the fires were several miles away from the camp area. Still, I thought it might be best to fly there after speaking with you and pick up Kyle right away."

"That would be wonderful, Hank," Julie said, her voice softening. "But what's all of this?" She waved her hand at the items strewn across the bed. "I've tried a number of times today to reach Kyle with no luck."

"Have you checked your computer since you realized your phone was missing?" Hank asked, sorting through his equipment. "The Scouts might have sent something out to parents. Or have you been too distracted?" He glanced up and wanted to bite his tongue, seeing the hurt flash in her eyes.

"That's low, Hank," she said. "And no, by the way. I was late getting home tonight and had promised Chris a movie and pizza."

He stopped and held her gaze. "Listen, I won't pretend that I don't have a ton of questions going through my mind right now, but it will have to wait. You and I...will have to wait."

"Hank, you're scaring me." She frowned. "What's the matter?"

"I tried to call to tell you that Pete called me back while I was en route here. It appears the winds have caused the fires to shift. Pete's team has been called up and are assembling at the Denver airport. I'm on my way there to meet up with them." He began stuffing things back in the bag.

"What about getting Kyle?" Julie asked.

"That's the problem. The fires are now moving toward the National Park and the Scout camp. They're calling in smokejumpers from all over to get it contained."

"Close to the camp," she repeated, as though it was taking root in her mind. "Is anyone doing anything?" She looked at him. "Have there been evacuations?"

Hank nodded. "Pete said the DNR has headed up the mountain to order mandatory evacuations for all campers. The firefighting teams are being dispatched to the impacted areas. There are apparently a few homes up in those mountains. They hope to be able to contain it before it reaches the area, but with the overly dry conditions, it's not looking good."

"I'm coming with you," she said suddenly, and turned to leave. "I'll get my things."

"No, Julie." Hank said. "That's not a good idea."

"Excuse me, that's *my* son up there." She had the look of an angry mother bear.

Any other time, he'd have conceded, but his frustration level was currently high.

"You have Chris *here*," he threw out, hoping it would make a difference.

"Clay can watch Chris," she argued.

"Julie," Hank warned, "you won't be able to do anything."

"And just what do you think *you're* going to do?" she asked.

Hank released a sigh. "I may be needed to fly some guys over the fires and drop them in."

Her gaze narrowed. "Give me your phone." She held out her hand.

Hank held her steady gaze.

"Hank, I swear. Give me your damn phone or I'll get in my car and start driving myself."

It was clear she wasn't going to budge and arguing would waste precious time. Shaking his head, he handed her the phone.

She called Clay who said he'd pick up Chris at the main house.

"I'll get my things," she said, handing the phone back.

The three-hour flight to Denver was worse than wisdom teeth removal—long, tension-filled, and mostly painful. What dialogue there was between them was stilted, uncomfortable. The concern of what the future held on so many levels was a major factor.

Hank was more than a little happy to see the Denver airport come into view.

A few moments later, he landed and hopped from the plane. Pete greeted him on the tarmac. The two friends embraced one another in a quick hug.

Julie walked up beside Hank.

"This is Julie, Kyle's mom. The boy I told you about," Hank said.

Pete glanced at him, a flash of curiosity in his eyes. "Hi, Julie. Just want you to know we'll do everything possible to find your son and get him and this guy back home safe and sound."

"Find...my son?" Julie glanced at Hank, then back to Pete. "What do you mean?"

"Did the DNR get up to the Scout camp?" Hank asked.

Pete nodded as he showed them a map on his tablet, pointing to the area where the Scout camp was located. "They did. We just got word that those in the camp have been notified of evacuations. However—"

"However?" Hank asked. His gut twisted.

"Part of the troop—eight boys and two leaders—

who'd gone on a survival hike are unaccounted for. We think they may have gotten cut off when the winds shifted."

"Shit," Hank muttered, and looked at Pete.

Julie's eyes were wide, filled with panic. "Has anyone heard from them?"

Pete held the tablet out, pointing to an area on the map. "We've got guys on the ground trying to keep this thing from heading over this ridge. The trail that I understand the boys would have taken follows along the canyon, near the river."

"We need to get moving," Hank said. "What do you need me to do?"

Pete tapped the screen, bringing up another view of the terrain. "My team is suited up and ready. The wind is not making this easy, but with any luck the river in its path will buy us some time." Pete nodded curtly. "That will be our chance to drop in and do some clearing before it gets there. Maybe keep it from jumping the river." He pointed to the neon-colored screen. "There's an abandoned airstrip once used by the DNR. We can drop down this ridge and work that side of the river. Do what we can to find them."

Hank nodded. He glanced at Julie, her fearful eyes fixed on the tablet. He placed his arm around her and kissed her temple. "We'll find them, Jules." She stood stoic at his side, hugging her arms.

"I've brought a friend of mine with me, Julie." Pete waved over a middle-aged woman who'd been passing out information sheets to the other members of his team. The woman had beautiful, cocoa-colored skin. Her warm, dark eyes looked

WORTH THE WAIT

at Julie.

"The latest updates have been passed out," the woman told Pete.

"Julie, this is Rosita. She's my right hand in the office. You go with her and you'll be updated as often as news comes in."

"Thank you, Pete," Julie said.

"You ready?" Pete looked at Hank.

"Ready."

"Good. The sooner we get those kids out of there, the better," Pete said.

Hank watched as Julie pressed her lips together, holding in every ounce of resolve. She'd been through a lot and, while it may have scarred her heart when it came to love, she was a fighter when it came to her kids. She looked at him, her eyes glistening. "You promise." She searched his eyes. "Promise me that you both will come back safe."

Hank squeezed her shoulder. "I promise," he said. He looked at Rosita, who took Julie's arm and gently led her to a waiting SUV.

Pete slapped Hank on the shoulder, jarring him from staring after Julie. He knew what he was going into. It wouldn't be easy. He had to keep his wits about him for the sake of these men, for Kyle and for Julie. The clock was ticking. He knew how fickle Mother Nature could be. Time was a precious commodity. "Let's get going."

"Pete felt it best if we waited here," Rosita said, handing Julie a hot cup of tea. They'd found a small table tucked in a private corner of a large connection of waiting rooms that overlooked the hospital's parking lot and emergency entrance. The area was sectioned off into several smaller, comfortable rooms with a variety of sofa and chair groupings. Artwork, a two-sided fireplace, a small coffee shop, and potted plants of every description offered a peaceful solace for those waiting long hours for surgeries or tests.

Rosita handed her a cup of hot tea that she'd gotten just before the small coffee shop closed for the evening. The waiting area was nearly empty except for an elderly couple sitting quietly next to the fireplace.

"I'll set up my laptop and keep my phone charged so we can stay current with what's going on out there," Rosita said. "Pete said he'd call with updates when he can."

"Thank you." Julie wrapped her fingers around the mug, clinging to its warmth.

"Try to drink it. It will help some," Rosita said. "Is Kyle your only son?" she asked, glancing up at Julie as she booted up her laptop. "Pete told me it was Kyle up at the camp." With expert efficiency, she had unwrapped and plugged in chargers for all her devices in record time.

Julie breathed in deeply the calming vapors of the honey-chamomile tea, attempting to quell her nerves. Her brain had been swirling between prayers to God and visions of Kyle, flames surrounding him. "I have another son, eighteen months younger. Chris is back home with my brother and his family."

Rosita nodded, listening as she focused on setting up the wildfire information website.

"Do you have children?" Julie asked. The

woman appeared young— younger than Julie, at any rate. Her skin was flawless, and she wore no makeup with her standard-issue gray T-shirt with the wildfire logo and slim-fitting jeans.

Julie was being polite, but the truth was she needed the distraction to keep her mind off worrying about Kyle and Hank.

"I did. One son." She looked up. "He was a wildfire fighter."

Was? Julie's concerns about Kyle faded a bit as she looked at the woman so in control, it seemed, of her emotions. Rosita, sensing perhaps Julie's inability to respond to the news, smiled—in the way a mother does when remembering a sweet memory.

"He loved his job and he was quite good at what he did. Pete had always said that he envisioned Jarod as his right-hand man one day." Rosita cleared her throat and took a sip of her tea.

Julie was more than a little afraid to ask what had happened. "Do you...want to talk about it?" Her few sessions with Reverend Cook had not yet afforded her with the belief that she held any storehouse when it came to her faith. She was learning that day-by-day. Sometimes, moment-by-moment.

Rosita stopped typing and her gaze focused on her tea bag. She dunked it slowly, seeming to take her time. "It was five years ago. He and his wife had just received news of their first child." She smiled at the memory. "He'd done hundreds of jumps..." She shook her head. "But this one, he landed badly, against a boulder. He suffered a head injury that he never recovered from. Two weeks he was on a resuscitator, and finally they told us we needed to let him go."

"Oh, lord, Rosita. I'm…" Sorry seemed too trite, but she could think of no other comforting words. "I'm so sorry."

Rosita looked down and Julie could see the woman fight to pull herself back from the pain of the memory. "He was a good man. Always had a bright smile. Loved life." Her brows pinched together, marring her otherwise serene features. "With all the bad people in the world, it makes you wonder why God would need to take one of the good ones home."

"And his family?" Julie asked.

Rosita smiled, a genuine light filling her eyes. "Conner and his mother live with me now. It is a blessing to see the little boy each day who reminds me so much of his father."

Julie regarded the woman, admiring her strength. She thought of her own experience. The emotional and later the physical abuse Louis had displayed. He'd never touched the boys, but if he had, Julie was fairly certain it'd be her sitting in a prison cell right now. "I'm surprised you're still able to work around all of this."

Rosita shrugged. "To be honest, I wasn't certain I could. I took some time away, of course. Then I realized that Pete, the other guys, their wives and children…we're all family. I feel closer to my son here than I do anywhere else."

Julie nodded. "I can't imagine what it's like, Rosita, but I know this—right now, it feels as though someone has taken my breath away. Until I know Kyle is safe, I can't breathe right."

WORTH THE WAIT

She nodded. "They'll find them. Pete's the best there is. And he has nothing but good things to say about Hank," Rosita said. "How'd you and Hank meet?" she asked.

Julie blinked, pulling from the fear that threatened to paralyze her at times, especially when she was under stress. She struggled to organize her thoughts. "He and my brother were friends in college." She looked at the woman across from her, a woman who had every right to be bitter, angry. And yet she was asking about Julie, making conversation and trying to stay positive. "They're still friends," she said, smiling at the realization of the solidarity of the friendship. Louis had forbidden her to become involved, or to make friends. The boys hadn't been allowed to have friends over to the house. He'd kept her to a tight schedule on the home front. In retrospect, what she regretted most was how her kids had suffered through her blindness.

"You mentioned earlier that your other son was with your brother. Do you live in the same town?" Rosita took a sip of her tea and grimaced. "Cold, yuck."

Julie spotted a pot of water warming at the coffee station. She held her hand out for Rosita's cup. "May I warm that up?"

The woman grinned. "You've had some practice waitressing, I see."

Julie nodded as she poured. "I do the books for the diner and bakery in End of the Line. Now and again, I fill in when someone is sick or can't get in due to the snow."

"So, you and Hank are settled in End of the

Line, then?" She nodded her thanks and dipped her tea bag in the water.

"It's complicated," she said, returning the pot. "And honestly, it's a boring story."

"Boring? Honey, this man is flying into God knows what to get your son. It doesn't sound too boring to me."

Julie sat down and folded her hands in front of her. "We just got engaged. Less than a month ago, actually."

"Well, that calls for congratulations." Rosita lifted her mug in salute. "When's the date?"

"The date?" Julie's mind was still working on her first question—meeting Hank.

She'd stood looking down at him as they prepped Hank to load him into the ambulance. In the flurry of the rescue, Louis had fired a shot meant for her. Hank had intervened and was hit just above the shoulder. The bullet nicked his clavicle bone, but thankfully had missed anything vital.

Hank had taken her hand and tried to smile through the pain. "I'll check in with you and the boys when they clear me to go."

She'd glanced over at her brother. She remembered Hank from the time she'd gone to watch Clay play football. He'd been a sweet guide and protector on campus—a duty he'd confessed to not having looked forward to at the time, but would later tell her that he believed had been fate.

"Okay, there, Captain America. I'm here, too, remember?" Clay had said, smiling at his friend.

"We'll discuss later what I meant when I said 'stick to the plan,' okay, buddy?"

She'd stood in stoic silence watching the array of squad cars and emergency personnel drive away. Curious neighbors had filtered outside to watch the drama unfold, the dark secrets of their "perfect" family revealed to all.

"Jules?"

She'd heard her brother's voice and felt her children's arms grip her tightly around the waist. Reality slammed into her and her knees buckled. Clay caught her, wrapping his arms around the three of them. "He won't hurt you guys ever again," Clay had said with quiet assurance.

Later that night after visiting Hank, relieved to know his injury wouldn't leave any residual physical damage, she'd remembered how kind he'd been to her. But hindsight was twenty-twenty. In college, she'd been infatuated with a promising young lawyer by the name of Louis Williams. Hank simply hadn't been her type. She marveled now at how blind she'd been.

Clay had pitched moving to Montana over coffee the next morning. "I think it'd be a good idea for you and the boys to move to End of the Line for a while," Clay had said. "The boys are going to need family, and the Last Hope Ranch is an ideal place to recuperate from all you guys have been through. Plenty of fresh air and working with the horses did wonders for me."

It hadn't taken much to convince her. She'd needed to be as far away from Louis as possible. She needed to make a new life for herself and the boys. She needed to be around family, and her boys would benefit from the same.

Little had she known how things would quickly change between her and Hank.

Julie blinked from her reverie. "We haven't had time to set a date yet." She glanced briefly away, then met Rosita's' steady gaze. Okay, it wasn't the complete truth, but she wasn't prepared to delve into the topic. Her thoughts were truly well muddled.

The woman held her gaze a moment and then went back to her laptop.

Taking the opportunity to find some time alone, she walked to the other end of the long room that looked over the parking lot and emergency entrance. Neon signs and street lamps had begun to pop on in the wake of the dusky, overcast skies. She thought of Kyle, wondering where he was, praying he was safe, praying he and the other boys would soon be found.

She glanced up at the sprinkling of stars and thought of Hank, of the argument they'd had before he left, the passion they'd shared…she smiled thinking of the moment when everything had changed between them.

They'd gone to Dusty's to celebrate three months of living in End of the Line. They'd agreed it wasn't a real date, just two friends sharing a couple of drinks. The shift had occurred when he'd asked her to dance. She'd refused at first, but in light of his persistence, she had finally

WORTH THE WAIT

surrendered.

He'd worn a blue plaid cowboy shirt that brought out the deep brown of his eyes. His cologne mingled with the heat from his body, an aphrodisiac for a woman craving the proper attention of a man. He'd held her close, swaying to the music, wrapping his fingers around hers. When she looked into his eyes, she saw that he, too, knew how well they would fit together.

All night, he'd been a gentleman—opening doors, asking how she and the boys were doing, then guiding her back to the booth, his hand resting softly on the small of her back. Being cared for in even such small ways was foreign to her, yet a balm to her bruised heart.

In retrospect, she'd admitted, as he had later, that the beer consumption had likely influenced the night, allowing the walls to come down. But neither had anticipated—at least, Julie hadn't—what would happen when he took her hand and led her to his truck.

It had been an explosion of pent-up desire. His kisses all but drowned her, pulling her under, making her never want to come up for air.

"The bakery," she'd managed to get out between hungry kisses—kisses that had made her want to throw all inhibitions aside.

The enclosed narrow stairway off the alley made it difficult to steal another kiss without stopping periodically. When at last they made it to the door, she turned and faced him. "There aren't any lights," she said. "The city inspector shut off the electricity."

He searched her eyes. "We don't need lights,

darlin'." He kissed her again, causing her head to spin.

"Only an old twin mattress," she whispered, breathless from the overwhelming need rising inside her.

"Are we trespassing?" he asked, his hands resting on her hips.

"I-I don't know. I have the key, so technically... no?" she said.

"When does Rebecca come in to bake downstairs?" he asked, moving so close that his body pressed hers against the door.

"Around four?" she said, and her head swirled with fantasies of what it would be like with him.

"It's two," he said. "We can call it a night, if you want."

She grabbed the front of his shirt. "Is that what you want?"

His response was a low, sexy chuckle. "Not by a long shot, darlin', but what do you want?"

She wasn't sure where this would end up in the long run—she only knew that to deny herself this one night would be wrong. She needed to be free, to release the emotions she boxed inside her all these months. She needed to *feel* again. She was tired of this numbness inside her, tired of being afraid to let another man touch her again.

She swallowed, relaxing her grip as she met his heated gaze. "You, Hank," she said. "It's just that its been so long...." She met his eyes. "I'm afraid."

His gaze softened and his smile warmed her to her toes. He reached up and gently brushed his knuckles down her cheek. "I don't want you to be afraid, Julie. I want to help you feel good, sweetheart." He kissed her softly, his lips skimming the side of her jaw. "You're a beautiful woman, Julie—inside and out. I've known that for a very long time."

She leaned her head to the side to accommodate his deliberations, closing her eyes to the delicious effects of his tender touch. Sex with Louis had never been gentle, never tender. With each pregnancy she'd hoped that he'd change and become more loving. Instead, after Chris he'd stayed later at work, took weekend meetings, and had little time for his family.

That twin mattress became Julie's rebirth in terms of being intimate with a man. He'd loved her with a reverence she'd never known, soothing her fears, gentle with his touch, until her body thrummed with need. Then he'd shown her what it was like to touch the stars.

What was thought to be a one-night stand instead opened a door between them—one heart searching to find herself after a tumultuous marriage, the other yearning to make this woman and her boys the family he'd always dreamt of.

A shrill buzzing noise brought Julie back to the present and she realized the tears that stained her cheeks were a result of the fortress she'd built around her heart beginning to crumble.

She loved him.

The simple truth of it surprised and delighted her.

"That was Pete," Rosita said, motioning for Julie to rejoin her. "He said the helicopters just dropped off the first round of Scouts at the airport, and they should be en route to the hospital by now. Parents have been notified to meet their kids here. If they are cleared by the doctors, they're allowed to go home." Julie realized that she'd missed that notification with her phone still back at the diner.

"Any news on Kyle?" Julie swiped away the tears her revelation had produced inside of her.

"He didn't say. Only that they were heading out to look for the small group that had gone out earlier on an adventure," Rosita said as she quickly collected her gear and stuffed it in her large canvas bag.

The sound of sirens accompanied by flashing lights came up the drive, splashing the room with red and blue. Julie looked out to see two medivac ambulances in tandem pulling under the ER canopy.

"Did he mention anything about Hank?" Julie asked as they hurried to the elevator that would take them downstairs.

"Only that he was waiting in the plane ready to transport," Rosita said. "He'd be in touch when possible. "You ready?" Rosita slung the bag over her shoulder. "Let's go see if your boy is with this group."

CHAPTER NINE

HANK WAS GLAD THE CAMP itself had been safely evacuated, but his gut told him that Kyle was likely among those who'd optioned for an adventure hike earlier in the day. He squinted into the smoky darkness, attempting to see the clearing through the haze and what little daylight was left.

He felt a tap on his shoulder and turned to find Pete leaning forward in his seat. "The abandoned airstrip is on top of that ridge. Think you can land this thing in a short distance in the dark?" his old friend asked. "We'll rappel down the cliff. It's getting dark and it'll be safer than trying to parachute in."

Hank nodded, and tipped the plane toward his destination. The area was remote. The fires blazing high on the ridge on the opposite side of the river cast an ethereal glow flickering against the shadowed canyon walls. Clearly, it was suitable only for experienced hikers and climbers.

"I've got the helicopters headed to the strip to bring in any injuries," Pete said, then glanced at the man he'd assigned as Hank's co-pilot. "Jack will stay with you."

Pete signaled to his men and they prepared to

unload the minute they landed.

Hank scanned the raging inferno on the horizon gobbling up the terrain. He had no idea of how skilled the young Scout leaders were, or if any of the boys had a lick of survival training, much less if they'd carried emergency-type equipment with them.

"That bitch looks hungry," Jack muttered, his focus on the same sight.

Hank looked at Jack. "Is there any way to find out if this group had equipment to climb if need be?"

"Copy that, sir. I'll see what I can find out," Jack said.

Hank spotted the airstrip, not much more than a swathe where trees had been cleared to make a short landing strip. One end was guarded by a dense forest of pine, the other a steep drop into oblivion. Beyond, a harsh red fury appeared to be eating everything in its path. They didn't have much time.

The strip was void except for a herd of frightened deer as Hank brought the plane down. He taxied to the end and brought the plane around in preparation for an immediate take-off. An empty communications tower stood off to one side—a dark, foreboding sentinel among the trees. He shut off the engine and stared into the dark abyss.

"Jack," Pete ordered, "let's set up some trip flares at the end of that runway. Get some light out there."

"Yes, sir," Jack said. "I was able to patch through and spoke to the main Scout headquarters in Denver. They said one of the leaders he spoke to indicated the boys were equipped with walkie-talkies, but they'd lost contact a couple of hours ago."

Hank stared at the smoldering horizon.

"Where was the last point of contact?" Pete asked.

Jack unfolded a map. "Not far from here. That's Diablo Creek that we flew over coming in."

"How long is it?" Hank asked, unbuckling from his seat.

"Runs along the canyon, probably seventy miles or so, then dumps into Crater Lake," Pete said.

Hank glanced at him. "I don't suppose there are any skilled climbers in that Scout group?" he asked.

Jack shook his head. "First-time Scout leaders. I'm guessing rock-climbing at the YMCA."

"It's possible, then, that they'd have some equipment," Pete interjected, slapping Hank on the shoulder. "We'll find them, Hank," his friend said.

The plane shook as the men tossed out their packs. Like large fireflies, Hank watched as each man broke open their flares and carried their gear toward the steep ledge overlooking the creek canyon.

The open door ushered in the smell of heavy smoke with the wind. The stench taunted Hank's patience. "What do we have back there?" he asked, unable to sit by quietly and wait.

Jack flipped through his clipboard. "We have first-aid kits, ropes, clamps, blankets, one sling, and one stretcher. The choppers will have better equipment and should be here any minute now."

Hank was growing antsy, just sitting there doing nothing. "You have an ETA on those guys?"

Jack spoke into one of his walkie-talkies, then turned to Hank. "ETA fifteen minutes."

The radio crackled and Hank heard Pete's voice. "We found a backpack. Looks like they headed for the ridge."

Hank stood and slapped Jack's shoulder. "Come on, let's get those flares up on the landing strip."

After igniting the flares, they walked back to the edge of the cliff. Below, the strip stick that had been tossed over the ridge glowed eerily in the shadows. Hank looked over at Jack. "Ask Pete to send up a flare where they found the backpack."

Jack made the request into his walkie-talkie and they waited. A few moments later, a flare shot high into the dusky sky. Jack responded in kind.

"Maybe someone will see the flares," Hank said, "and know people are on the ground searching for them."

"Good idea, sir," Jack said.

Hank looked across the canyon, seeing that the fire had come over the opposite ridge. If the winds shifted again, it could bring it racing down toward the river in a heartbeat. "How many lanterns do we have, and those giant glow-sticks?" Hank asked.

"We have a couple of power lanterns and a bag of trip sticks back in the plane," Jack answered.

"Let's get some lights out here on this ridge. I want to see what they're up against. Maybe there's an easier climb somewhere along the face."

As they were checking the ridge, helicopters arrived and, with them, additional equipment and manpower.

Jack stayed in contact with Pete and continued to try various frequencies, hoping to reach the walkie-talkies the Scouts were reported to have.

Emergency rescue teams dropped several lines over the cliff. Pete and his men, who had spread out and started at the river, were now walking back toward the ridge. Below, Hank could see the lights of their helmets bobbing through the trees. There'd been no word on anything since they found the backpack.

Hank paced the ridge, periodically shining a periscopic flashlight down into the forest, hoping to catch a response from below.

"Hank," Jack called. "Over here. I think I have something."

Hank huddled near the walkie-talkie, straining to hear through the static.

"Is anyone out there?" said the disembodied, weary voice. "My dad is Hank Richardson."

Hank's heart leapt in his chest at the sound of Kyle's voice. He reached for the walkie-talkie. "Kyle, buddy, it's Hank. Listen, we've got guys on the ground looking for you. Can you tell me where you are?"

His answer was choppy at best, but Hank was able to make out *broken leg* and *in a cave*.

"Kyle, do you guys have a flare gun?" Hank asked.

"Will check." More static. Then only silence.

Jack had splayed a map on the ground, pinpointing the possibilities of where the cave might be.

"We need to get down there," Hank blurted out in frustration.

"Sir, my men are trained in these situations. Let us handle it," one of the EMTs said.

The shoe was now on the other foot. Hank knew the man was right. He hadn't had a refresher course in his training. There was little he could do but say a prayer and wait. Still, it didn't do a damn thing to lessen his frustration of wanting to be down there himself.

"Flare about eighty yards to the right, sir," one of the rescue crew shouted.

Hank offered up a silent prayer of thanks.

"Winds are shifting. We've got to move," called out another crew member.

Pete's voice crackled over the walkie-talkie. "I'll send my guys over the river, see if we can clear out and buy some time."

Hank wanted to shout that it was too dangerous, but in his next breath he knew that's exactly where he'd be if he could.

One by one, the members of the rescue team rappelled down the ridge with remarkable agility into the increasing heat and smoke.

Hank, Jack, and the other pilots stood watching the trail of lights weaving through the trees. They'd taken air masks, first aid equipment, and two stretchers, having no idea what they might find.

After what seemed an eternity but in reality was a relatively short amount of time, the first of the rescue crews began to appear over the ridge. The Scouts that could manage were hoisted up in chair slings. Hank assisted the dehydrated Scouts to the helicopters, where they were given blankets and water.

WORTH THE WAIT

He'd started counting—first two, three, then four boys were pulled up the ledge. He looked up and noticed gray ash beginning to snow down on them. The winds had shifted, blowing embers over the river. They were running out of time.

He caught the arm of one of the men on the rescue team who'd brought up another boy. "How many are left?" he asked over the roar of one of the helicopters about to take off. The boys would be transported to Denver airfield where ambulances were on stand-by to take them on to the hospital.

"Four at the base. Two in the cave. We only have two stretchers— both being used for the injured. They're coming up now. We have a fracture in the cave. Have to give 'em credit—the splint those boys made probably saved his leg."

Hank sighed. All he could do now was watch and wait. The team was meticulous, slow and steady bringing the stretcher up the cliff face. First one and then the other stretcher was unhooked from the ropes. Other members of the team carried the baskets to the waiting helicopter. He'd checked on each boy, hoping to see a familiar face.

Neither was Kyle.

The smoke had begun to thicken as the team rappelled once more down the cliff.

Jack, whom Hank hadn't seen in a while, handed him a bandana. "Put it over your mouth and nose," he said. "It'll help some. You don't want to breathe in this shit."

He nodded. He knew in his gut that Kyle was likely one of the two left down there—maybe the one with the broken leg.

He stood on the cliff's edge, willing the fire to back away from the rescue team. With one swift breeze, those below would have little chance of survival. The ones above would have to take off over a raging inferno.

He heard his name and shined his light down to the base where he was glad to see Pete, his crew close behind.

The other team came through the trees. Between them, they sent up another stretcher. The person lay motionless, his face obscured by a breathing mask and black soot, making identification difficult.

"Hank!" came a high-pitched yell.

He turned and ran toward Kyle, who was scrambling out of the harness. Hank pulled him int his arms and held him close despite the boy's heavy coughing.

"You need to go, Hank." Pete untangled himself from the web of rope and carabiners.

"Let's get these people on board," called one of the rescue team leaders.

"Leave everything, let's go," Pete yelled to his crew.

Hank steered Kyle toward the waiting helicopter. "You need to go with these folks and let them check you over."

"I want to go with you," Kyle said, but his voice kept getting lost in the fray of urgent orders being called out around them.

"I'll see you at the hospital. Get up there." He lifted him onto the helicopter.

Kyle started to protest. "I don't need to go to the hospital."

"Your mom is waiting there, worried sick. Now get in that seat. Let the medics check you out and I'll see you later."

"Promise?" he asked.

That stopped Hank. The boy broke free from the medic's care and threw himself into Hank's arms.

"Okay, buddy. It's going to be okay. I'll see you soon," Hank said, helping him back into the helicopter.

Jack tugged on Hank's arm as Kyle settled in and buckled up.

"It's going to swallow the valley. We need to go," Jack said.

The medivac helicopter took off. A third had landed to take Pete and his team to another location to meet up with another division of firefighters. Jack looked at Hank as he buckled in. "Piece of cake," he said with a grin.

Hank noticed the first narrow bands of light beginning to peek over the mountains, shrouded by dense smoke. He started the engines and began rolling down the narrow runway. The light grew brighter, dancing along the edge of the ridge. There was no way until they were off the ridge to know how intense the fire was below, how high the flames rose.

As Hank brought the engines to full throttle, he saw Jack cross himself.

Hank's body was drenched in sweat, his skin covered with soot. Fear, but a greater determination to survive—to see Julie and the boys again—drove him.

The nose dipped slightly, offering a clear, panoramic view of the lake of fire below. He pulled up, fighting the heat and the crosswind caused by the fire. The plane jerked from right to left. His arms ached from gripping the controls. His jaw muscles twitched as he fought to get more altitude.

"How are we doing, Jack?" he asked, his back teeth grinding from the force of his determination.

"Good, just a minor complication," Jack answered, as he glanced out his window. "We've got a fiery branch sucked into one of the engines." Just then the propeller slowed to a complete stop.

The sputtering started, and it rattled the plane. "We need to set her down. Any ideas?" Hank asked, his heart dwindling as he looked over the glowing sea of red.

Jack took out the map. "There's a lake not far from here. It might be our only chance."

"Sounds like a deal," Hank said. "Anything is better than blowing up in the sky, right?"

"Agreed." Jack pointed to the lake. "There it is." Surrounded by mountains, it was formed like a giant crater had dropped onto the earth.

"At least the fire is behind us," Hank said with a wry grin.

"You can do this, sir," Jack said, flipping switches and checking the view in front of them.

"This isn't going to be pretty." Hank slowed his engines in order to coast in and hopefully soften the landing. "You know how to swim?"

"On my college swim team," Jack said, turning to Hank with a wide grin.

Hovering over the lake, the distance between

plane and black water closed in at a rapid pace. The plane hit the surface, spraying water into the air with the force akin to hitting a freight train head-on. Hank's body, pushed forward by the force, slammed into the controls. He felt a quick snap in his side before the front window imploded and knocked him back in the seat. Frigid water rushed over him. He only had time to glance over at Jack, who was doubled over, his chin dropped against his chest. *I'm sorry, Kyle,* was his last thought before his world went black.

Julie stood near the emergency room entrance, pressed against the wall as gurney after gurney was rolled in from the ambulance. Most of the Scouts had oxygen masks over their faces; some had IV's already attached to their arms.

She searched the faces of each boy, sharing in the elation and relief as waiting parents spotted their child and followed them into the bay of observation rooms.

Another ambulance arrived, bringing a rush of ER personel to help with a man suffering from a heart attack. Another man wheeled his wife, in pronounced labor, through the entrance, searching frantically for a doctor.

Julie watched the flurry of activity going on in the massive emergency room. She and Rosita found a couple of chairs and waited. It was more than twenty minutes later before two more ambulances arrived, bringing in additional Scouts. She scanned the faces as best she could as they were rushed past, their bodies covered by blankets, their exposed skin covered in ash and soot.

A gurney rolled past her, and it was Kyle who noticed her first. He reached up his hand. "Mom," he called out with a raspy voice that sounded nothing like her son.

Julie grabbed his hand and followed him in as they swung the gurney around and placed him on a bed.

"Ma'am, we need you to move back until we've had a chance to get him stable," a nurse said, taking her arm and gently leading her to the door.

Kyle was coughing hard. He clawed at the oxygen mask.

"Can he breathe?" she asked out loud, then realized she needed to force herself to let these people do their jobs. She stepped back into the hall where a large window separated the curtained observation rooms.

Rosita followed her in from the waiting room, joining her in the hallway. "Is that Kyle?" she asked.

Julie nodded, mentally assessing how he'd looked on the gurney, how he'd sounded. "Yes. He was able to speak to me, but he didn't sound like himself."

"They brought in another guy after you left—he had a broken leg. I overheard the EMTs praising the Scouts for quick thinking in splinting his leg."

Julie's heart swelled with pride. She looked at Rosita. "Has there been any word from Pete?"

Her new friend nodded. "He said that he and the team took a chopper to meet up with another division. Sounds like they're making headway with containing this fire."

"And Hank?" Julie asked.

"He and Jack—one of our guys—took off just after the others. Jack will drive them straight here in one of our trucks when they land at the airport."

Julie watched the flurry of medical providers, teams of them working room-to-room, checking on the Scouts. She spied a man dressed in a long white coat, his face solemn, walk into her son's room.

A moment later he walked past her and she reached out, touching his arm. "Excuse me?" she asked. "That's my son you just saw. Can you tell me what's happening?"

The man adjusted his glasses and checked the clipboard he carried. "I was called down to advise on x-rays. I'm sorry, the nurse will brief you when she has time."

She nodded. "Thank you," she said, watching as he entered another room.

"Julie?"

She turned and found a fresh-faced young woman also holding another clipboard.

"Yes, I'm Julie Williams. Kyle is my son. Is he going to be okay?"

The nurse took her by the elbow and guided her to one side. "Your son is in remarkable shape considering what he's been through. But the doctor felt it was a good idea to get some x-rays to see how much damage has been done to his airways and lungs."

"Can you…treat this?" she asked, accepting the clipboard the woman handed her.

She nodded. "With proper treatment, the body

is quite resilient. His age gives him an advantage. But we do need you to sign the consent form to take him upstairs."

Julie signed where the woman instructed and then was directed to go down to admissions to provide insurance information so Kyle could be admitted.

"He's going to be with us for a few days, at least," the nurse said.

Julie and Rosita took care of getting her son's paperwork processed, had a bite of breakfast in the cafeteria while awaiting Kyle's x-rays, and were now back in the emergency waiting room.

A hacking cough brought Julie's head up, and she saw Pete striding across the room. He looked tired, his face still smudged with ash and soot. He pulled off the bandana from around his neck and wiped his face. "How's Kyle?" he asked.

"Still up in radiology," Julie said. "They're checking his lungs. The nurse says he's going to be here a few days. He was severely dehydrated—as they all were, I imagine. Have you been in touch with Hank?"

Pete's gaze, a startling blue in his soot-covered face, studied her. "He and Jack aren't here?" He pulled out his cell phone, quickly skimming his messages before punching in one number, and then another. He frowned. "Both numbers go straight to voicemail."

"What does that mean, exactly?" Julie asked. Her boys were better at understanding the nuances of technology than her.

Pete shrugged. "Any number of things, really," he said in the vaguest way possible.

WORTH THE WAIT

"Pete, just say what's on your mind," she said.

"It's odd. I saw them take off just after we did." He glanced at his watch. "Maybe I'll call the tower and see if they've heard from him."

He stepped away, and in the next room, Julie could hear the crackle of the radio walkie-talkie. A moment later, Pete returned, his face grim. "He hasn't landed or radioed in."

Julie closed her eyes against the panic clawing to make its way out. He had to be okay. They had a lot of things to talk out, to resolve. She had to tell him how much she cared and adored him…how she realized that she truly loved him. Her insides ached. She felt as though she'd been kicked by a horse.

"Mrs. Williams?" A different nurse, dressed in bright yellow scrubs, smiled at her. "If you'll follow me, I'll take you up to your son now."

Julie shot a look at Pete.

He placed his hands on her shoulders and held her gaze. "Take care of Kyle. I'll find Hank." He looked at Rosita.

"I'll keep trying Jack's cell phone," she said.

Pete nodded and looked back at Julie. Leaning forward, he gave her a quick peck on the forehead. "I'll find him."

Soon after Pete left, Julie borrowed Rosita's phone and called Clay as they followed the nurse through a maze of hallways.

"Thank goodness they found those kids," he said after she'd briefed him on what little she knew. "Have you seen Kyle?"

He and Chris were en route to Denver, along with Dalton to help with the driving. There were many who wanted to come, but it simply wasn't feasible. With Aimee due anytime now, Wyatt, Rein, and Liberty were on standby. Though Chris wanted Emilee to ride along, she'd stayed at home to help her mom with her young brother.

"I'm about to go in and seem him. They did x-rays, checking for possible damage caused by smoke inhalation," she told her brother.

"You tell him his Uncle Clay has Chris and Uncle Dalton and we're on our way there," Clay said. "How's Hank?"

A lump rose quickly in Julie's throat. "He hasn't checked in. Pete was just here and he can't reach him by phone."

"That's odd," Clay said. "He called, probably four hours ago at least…it was his number, anyway, but it disconnected before I could answer."

"I'm worried. Pete said he and the co-pilot took off just after the helicopters. That's been several hours now," she said. "Pete's gone back out to try to see what he can find out."

"Try not to worry, Jules. How much sleep have you had?" Clay asked.

Julie's brain felt numb—she'd been running on adrenaline. She'd dozed a time or two while in the waiting room, but she'd had no adequate rest. She took a deep breath and stuffed her hand in her pocket as they followed the nurse to Kyle's room.

She felt the small pocketknife. Pulling it out, her memory was catapulted back to the moment Emilee had found it while in the backyard, and the reaction she'd had to it. "Clay, could you put me on speaker so I can say hello to Chris?"

"Hey, Mom. How are you doing? How's Kyle?"

her young son asked.

"I'm getting ready to go in and see him. I'll tell him you're on the way," she said. Tears threatened her composure as she realized how fragile life was. It'd been a hard lesson to learn, that you shouldn't waste a moment in telling your loved ones what they meant to you. "I love you, baby."

"Love you more, Mom. Uncle Dalton's going to get us there in a flash," Chris said.

She heard the glee in her son's voice. "Yes, well, Uncle Dalton better make sure that you all get here in once piece," she warned with a smile.

"Only going five miles an hour over the speed limit, Julie," she heard Dalton say.

Julie glanced at the knife in her palm. "Dalton, may I ask something about Emilee?"

"Sure," he said.

"Her visions. Are they...." Julie didn't want to insult the child's special abilities, but she was curious as to how often she was right with them.

"Accurate?" Dalton filled in the blank where she couldn't seem to find the right words.

Julie turned the knife over and over in her palm. Deep down, she had a feeling she knew the answer. "Pretty accurate, huh?"

"It's a gift passed every other generation on the maternal side. Rebecca's mother was a seer. Rebecca has the gift, but it's kept mostly to her dreams. Emilee seems to be able to hold an object and see things—in the past and the future. Honestly, I'm still trying to understand it myself. But I'm no longer a skeptic, I'll give you that much." There was a pause. "Why do you ask?"

Julie hesitated. "She found a pocketknife in

the backyard. It was Hank's, given to him by his grandfather, and he'd given it to Kyle when he became a Scout."

"Was it a specific vision?" Dalton asked.

"She said it was dark. Hard to tell since it'd been touched by more than one person."

"That could be a lot of things, Julie," he said.

"Sure, you're right," she said. "Okay. I've got to get in to see Kyle. I'm sure he's exhausted and will want to get some rest. We'll see you in a few hours. Please," she begged, "drive safe."

"See you soon, Jules," Clay said.

"Tell Kyle I'm bringing our Nintendo Switch," Kyle said. "Uncle Clay said we'd have to get permission from you and the doctor to play, though."

"I'll let it be a surprise, then. How's that?" Julie said. She smiled as she pocketed the knife. "Love you guys."

"Love you," came a varied male chorus in return.

CHAPTER TEN

*H*ANK HAD NEVER SEEN ANYTHING *so beautiful as the woman standing at the end of the aisle, preparing to walk between the rows of white chairs that had been set up on the spacious green lawn. He stood at the other end, under a gazebo festooned with grapevine and autumn flowers. The sky was a crystalline blue, the air crisp on this fresh autumn morning. His groomsmen stood to his left, the pastor to his right. His bride, dressed in a tea-length ivory gown, smiled at the two boys as they crooked their arms to escort her down the aisle.*

Several of their family and friends were there. Dabbing their eyes, smiling, taking pictures—everyone seemed jubilant on this special day. And he was the happiest groom that had ever lived.

It was the happiest day of his life.

All at once there was a loud rumble, a roar so loud that it drowned out the chaos and shouting. He stood watching the horrific scene unfold before him as an enormous black wave of water crashed over everyone, everything, sweeping them all into oblivion.

He wanted to cry out, but his body was numb, his throat constricted.

"We've got a pulse," came a voice he didn't recognize. The sense of floating turned into excruciating pain—pain that had him wanting to go back to the blissful state. Though he tried to breathe, it was as though an elephant sat on his chest. He tried to see, but he wasn't able to open his eyes. They felt heavy, swollen, caked with something cool and wet—mud, perhaps, or... was that blood? He tried to lift his hand, but had no strength.

"Get that stretcher over here," the voice ordered.

An image of darkness swallowing him whole slammed into Hank's brain. He tried to wiggle his fingers to get their attention. There was so much noise. The *thump-thump* of a propeller from overhead, another voice barking out orders. It felt as though his brain had been placed in a blender and nothing made sense.

"I'm here, buddy. I got you," the voice said.

Hank struggled to recognize it, but his mind saw only darkness.

"We're getting ready to send you and Jack to the hospital," said a man's voice close to Hank's ear. His head buzzed. He wanted to sleep.

"Hang in there, Hank," the man said.

He called me Hank. Why didn't that sound familiar? Still, he did what he could, which was wiggle his fingers to acknowledge he'd heard him.

Soon after, he felt his body being lifted onto a hard surface. Then, it seemed he was floating. A cool breeze brushed over his face and he felt a stinging sensation. The straps binding his arms rubbed against his torso, exacerbating the pain in his body as the stretcher twisted and turned in the breeze. He tried to remember what had happened. Where was he that he was being air-lifted to a helicopter? The basket jostled, and then it was pulled out of the wind. Something was jabbed into his arm, a mask was placed over his nose and mouth, and at last he succumbed again to the peace of darkness.

Hank fought to look away from the sharp, bright light. It felt like a laser burning his pupil. On the upside, at least he could open his eyes now...or maybe someone helped him with that task. The light swung to the other eye. Equally as bright. Equally as painful.

"Glad to see some fight in you," a man said.

The annoying light went away, replaced by the intense glow of the sun coming in through the window. He raised his hand to block the searing light and noticed the IV tube attached to the back of his hand. His tongue felt thick, his throat parched. A quick glance at his other arm brought the relief that at least it was still attached.

"Let me close the blinds. That should help some."

The voice sounded familiar. Not unpleasant. He offered a grateful sigh as the light diminished and the room dimmed. From the shadows walked the woman who'd provided the relief. She stood by his bedside and smiled down at him.

"I'm very happy to see you awake," she said.

She wasn't the only one. He attempted a smile, but he was too tired. She was a lovely woman and very kind. He glanced around the room, deducing he was in a hospital, then looked back at her. She looked like no nurse he'd ever seen in her faded denim jeans, a soft blue T-shirt, and a comfy looking sweater that hung to her knees.

"Are you thirsty?" she asked, then offered him a glass with a bendable straw. Her hands were delicate, her nails neatly trimmed and without polish.

He leaned forward to grasp the straw with his lips and a sharp pain stabbed his ribcage, traveling with lightning speed until it exploded in his brain.

He groaned and lay back on the pillows, wondering where he was and what freight train had hit him.

"You broke three ribs," the woman told him. "And you've already had one surgery to suture some pretty bad wounds on your leg and chest." She seemed to be studying him. "The doctors say you are a very lucky man." She reached for his hand and he flinched, pulling it away from her grasp.

"Hey, there he is."

Catching only a glimpse of the hurt that flashed through her eyes, he turned toward the male voice, hoping this would be someone he knew. Two men walked in, burly-looking guys with broad shoulders. One wore a faded, standard-issue gray T-shirt with the word "Army" emblazoned across the chest, and the other a black T-shirt, dark blue jeans, and a faded Cubs baseball cap. The biceps on these guys were impressive. He noticed one of them had a slight limp.

The woman looked at the men. "Where's Chris?"

"With Kyle," the gray-shirted man said, giving her a quick glance. "Safe and sound playing their game. Figured he wasn't going anywhere."

He looked at Hank. "Thought we'd come up here and see how *Trouble* is doing." He grinned and tapped the side of Hank's leg...his good leg, thankfully.

He watched as the man with the limp walked over and hugged the woman as though they knew each other very well, and then looked down at Hank. "You've actually looked a lot worse, you know." He grinned. "You are one lucky guy."

Hank tried to place the man, but his mind kept drawing a blank. He tried to smile, but felt a tug on his flesh. Reaching up, he discovered a swathe of gauze over his cheek that hindered his ability to smile. Which was ironic. He wanted to laugh out loud and tell these people he had no clue who they were.

"What's happened to him?" Julie asked as she and Clay sat in the family lounge and visited with Hank's doctor at Denver General. Dalton had gone back to check on Chris and Kyle, maybe take Chris for a bite to eat in the cafeteria.

"We believe it's a temporary amnesia. Caused most likely by the trauma of the implosion of glass and the velocity of the crash itself on the head and neck. From the reports we've gotten, it sounds as though they had been able to slow the plane down—which is good—but they still hit that water pretty hard. Based on what I've been told, both men are very lucky to still be here."

"How long do you think he'll be like this?" Julie asked.

"That depends. It could be a few days, a month,

maybe longer." The doctor looked from Clay to Julie. "His brain needs time to heal. Along with his physical injuries, he's suffered a tremendous trauma psychologically."

"Will we be able to take him home?" Julie asked. "Even if he still doesn't remember everything after he's released from the hospital?"

She felt Clay take her hand and give it a squeeze.

"The brain is still a mystery to modern science," the doctor said. "I wish I could give you guarantees. But the truth is, we'll just have to be patient and see."

Hank woke from another strange dream. He'd been flying in a lavender-hued sky, as ribbons of pink and purple on the horizon quickly turned into flames that licked the sides of the plane. The sound of the fire roared in his ears. He fought the controls, and then everything plunged into darkness.

He squinted, focusing on the pretty blonde who'd entered his room. Today, she wore jeans with a pastel-yellow sweater that buttoned up over a camisole beneath. Two young boys followed in behind her.

"Good morning, Hank. I brought you some visitors," she said with a bright smile.

He cleared his throat, but it still felt like a wad of cotton was stuck in his airways. "What day is it?"

"It's Thursday," she said.

Hank frowned. "How long have I been here?"

She seemed to study him. "You've been here since a week ago Saturday."

He blinked, confused by the passage of time. He rubbed his forehead. "I suppose like Doc said, my memory will come back, eventually."

Her smile was kind. He'd gotten used to seeing her when he rolled out of his state of perpetual dozing. His head hurt less when he closed his eyes. Today was better, but he still didn't recognize these people, even though he knew the woman's name was Julie and her friends were Clay and Dalton.

"Well," she said, "these are my boys, Kyle and Chris."

"Hello, boys. Have we met?" he asked them. He caught the uncertain glances they gave their mom.

"Uh, yeah," said Chris, the younger boy. "You've been dating our mom for a while now. Did you forget?"

Hank glanced at Julie. "It's possible. At least, that's what I've been told. Your mom seems like a really nice lady."

Chris's expression crumpled into a curious frown.

The older boy looked directly at him. "We came to say goodbye. I got released today and Uncle Clay is taking us back home."

Hank wished he knew where his home was. "So, you've been in the hospital, too?" he asked.

The boy glanced at his mom, then looked at Hank. "They say you don't remember some stuff. But I couldn't leave without thanking you."

"Thanking me?" Hank asked.

Kyle nodded. "Yeah, for coming to get me," he said. "I don't know what would've happened if you hadn't called your friend Pete. I mean, if it wasn't so scary, I'd say it was pretty awesome seeing all those choppers and rescue guys." He offered Hank a shy grin. "Managed to get my first-aid badge and survival badge, though."

Pete? Rescue choppers? It all sounded vaguely familiar. Images of his dream, the orange glow surrounding him, flashed through his thoughts. He eyed the boy, fighting to remember.

The boy then pulled out a small pocketknife and held it up with a grin. "Mom said Emilee found this in the yard. It must have fallen out while I was mowing. I promise I'll be more careful with it from now on."

His gaze held on to the wood-and-pearl-handled knife. He recognized it as the one his grandfather had given him. "Hey, where'd you find my lucky pocketknife?" he asked.

"Yes," Julie said, her eyes suddenly alive. "Do you remember giving it to Kyle when he became a Boy Scout?"

New images flashed through his mind, most of them a blur except for a ceremony of some sort— yes, a Scout ceremony. He remembered then the young boy's face when he opened the box. "I gave it to Kyle." He blinked, then looked at Julie. "Is this Kyle?"

Julie nodded. Her beautiful blue eyes glistened with unshed tears.

One by one, the locks keeping his memories imprisoned began to unlock—memories that had been just beyond his reach.

Two men had entered the room, standing off to one side watching him, as they all were.

WORTH THE WAIT

Hank's eyes darted from one person to another. There was Julie, his fiancée, Clay, his soon-to-be brother-in-law, and Dalton, his friend since college. He squeezed his eyes shut to allow the sudden rush of memory to settle in his brain.

He opened his eyes then, and immediately recognized Kyle. He held out his hand. "Oh, Jesus, Kyle, are you okay, buddy?"

The two boys split up, hurrying to either side of his bed.

He took their hands. "I am *really* glad to see you guys." Both draped their arms over him, and he winced as they hugged him.

He looked at Julie, who stood silently with tears streaming down her face. She gave him a wobbly smile.

He'd noticed Dalton duck out of the room.

The boys stepped back to allow their mom to step forward. She leaned down and cupped his face gently. "Do you remember now?" she asked.

He searched her tear-stained face. "I remember...I remember how much I love you."

"Oh," she said, her voice cracking with emotion. She buried her face in his shoulder, and he pressed his face into her hair. The familiar scent smelled like home.

"Good to have you back, Hank," Clay said, his grin wide.

Dalton returned with a doctor and nurse in tow. He walked around to the other side of the bed and took Hank's hand. "It's great to see you back to your old self, man," he said.

Hank's body hurt, but he was grateful to be alive. "What's great is to have my brain functioning properly again," he said with a grin.

Hank frowned and looked at Clay. "Where's my friend, Pete?" Hank realized suddenly he'd also had a co-pilot with him. "Jack? Where's Jack? And my plane…we had to go down in the lake. Did they recover my plane?"

"Okay, now, son. Let's slow things down a bit, how about?" The doctor, who'd been checking his pulse, listened to his breathing, and then pulled out a small penlight.

"I hate that thing," Hank said as the doctor gestured for him to lay back on the pillow.

"If you'd look to the right, please. Thank you. Now left. Good." He stepped back and seemed to study Hank. "Can you tell me what year this is?"

Hank thought a moment, then shrugged. "2018."

"Can you tell me where you live?" the doctor asked, writing all this down on a clipboard.

Hank cleared his throat again. "Currently, I live in Chicago, but I hope to remedy that in the not-too-far future." He glanced at Julie. "This is my fiancée, Julie. She and her boys live in End of the Line, Montana."

The doctor nodded with a smile. "Very good. It seems you are well on your way to getting back your full memory. Welcome back, Mr. Richardson."

"Oh, Doc. There was another man who came in when I did. My co-pilot, Jack? How is he?" Hank asked.

"He's going to be here a bit longer, but I feel confident that he'll make a full recovery. I understand that he was the one who got you to shore after the crash."

"Champion swimmer in college, he told me," Hank said. He still couldn't remember the details of how Jack had gotten them both to the rocky shore. But the first chance he got, he planned to find out. "When might I be able to see him?" he asked.

The doctor raised his brows. "We'll see how you're doing in a few days. How about that?" He glanced at Julie. "Congratulations on your engagement."

Later that evening, Hank sat in the recliner for the first time since his arrival, glad to be upright, glad to be alive, and more than a little grateful to have his memory back.

Julie walked in carrying a beautiful vase of flowers. She sat them on the wide window sill along with an array of plants from his parents, sister, and the Kinnsion families. "These are from Betty, Jerry, and everyone at the diner and bakery," she said, perching on the edge of the bed. "Oh, and exciting news. Aimee's in labor. Clay called to tell me. They're about halfway back home and stopping with the boys for the night. They said to get better so you can come home." She smiled and reached out to take his hand. "We've a lot to be thankful for, haven't we?"

He couldn't agree more.

"When I think that I might have lost both you and Kyle—" she started, then breathed deeply and tried to smile past another round of tears.

"But you didn't, baby. Come over here," he said, tugging on her hand. He pulled her into his lap.

"I don't want to hurt you," she said, not fully

letting her weight rest on his legs.

He brushed the hair from her face. "Jules, you've no idea how good I feel right now." He searched her eyes. "God, I love you." He touched her cheek.

She pressed her lips into a thin line, then smiled. He could see she was fighting tears. "I love you *so* much." She pressed a tender kiss on his lips. "Hank, I've been so blind, so scared, unable to believe that I could find a man like you."

He offered her a lopsided grin. There was a twinkle in his dark eyes. "And what kind of a man is that?" he asked.

She brushed the hair from his forehead. "Kind and loving, smart and brave. A man who loves my boys as much as I do. A man who wants us to be a family—a real family."

"You might have forgotten devastatingly handsome." He grinned.

"That goes without saying," she said, sliding her thumb over his lower lip. "It's going to take a lifetime to show you how much I care about you—how much I love you. I don't know how I'm going to be able to show you adequately."

He offered her an ornery grin and felt the tug of the stitches healing on his cheek, noting that he'd likely have a rugged scar when this was all said and done. But that wasn't at the forefront of his mind just now. "I can think of no less than a dozen suggestions," he said. "But until there's no risk of someone coming through that door and interrupting us, I guess you could tell me that you're ready to marry me."

She cradled his face in her hands and kissed him,

proving without a shadow of a doubt that all his man parts were in perfect working order.

"Just as soon as we can get everything arranged," she said.

He pushed her knees to either side of his hips, inching his hands beneath the hem of her shirt as he held her gaze.

"May I suggest a simple wedding, then?"

"Agreed," she said, leaning forward to meet his mouth in a searing kiss.

Julie looked up and her heart stopped. "Mother of pearl," she muttered aloud. She watched as Hank nodded to the various members of the diner's staff, ignoring their raised brows and appreciative smiles as he walked toward her office tucked in the corner of the diner's back room.

He wore a crisp, white dress shirt, dark blue Wranglers, and boots topped off with a tailored-to-fit black gentlemen's coat that hit him at the hip. All that was missing was a black Stetson. That, he carried in his hand until he reached her. He stood on the other side of her desk and plopped it on his head. "Good day, ma'am." He gave a nod.

Julie felt just a tad weak in the knees. And she was sitting down.

"My goodness, don't you look mighty sharp, Mr. Richardson," Betty said, assessing him from head-to-toe. She'd just brought the morning receipts to Julie. Business had picked up in the past few days with the Frontier Days weekend fast approaching.

"I have to agree," Julie said. She stood and

rounded the desk. Clamping her hands down on her hips, she looked him over. "I may just have to marry you," she said, scooting up on her tiptoes to kiss him. The wedding, just a few weeks away, couldn't come soon enough.

"You like it? Dalton helped me pick it out." He turned once and tipped the brim of his hat as he looked over his shoulder, giving her a sexy grin.

She considered taking the rest of the day off... but things were busy at the diner and already Betty had called in extra help. Instead, she slid her arms around his waist. "Cowboy, take me away," she said softly.

He slipped his arms around her and drew her into another slow kiss. "How are the reception plans coming?" he asked Betty when the kiss ended.

"The menu is all planned," Betty said. "No worries."

"And you're sure that it's okay the weekend after Thanksgiving?" Julie asked. She and Betty had been over the topic more than once in recent days.

Betty waved away Julie's concerns. "The diner is closed anyway. And I can't think of a better way to spend a holiday weekend than celebrating you two *finally* getting married."

Hank gave Julie a squeeze. "Dalton told me that Wyatt, Clay, and some of the folks from church are handling getting the barn ready for the reception. Liberty wanted to help, but she and Rein need to enjoy this time with their new family."

"A little girl," Betty gushed. "Can you believe it? Little Cody must be thrilled to have a new baby sister." She waved her hand again to collect her thoughts. "Rebecca and Emilee have been handling the decorations. I hear they are going to be beautiful."

Julie released a sigh of relief, glad she'd relinquished reception responsibilities to Betty. It was her wedding gift to them both, she'd told them, and they weren't about to argue.

"Sounds like everything is clicking along in End of the Line," Hank said with a chuckle. "And with any luck, we'll get through the Frontier Days festival and this wedding before the snows come in."

Julie glanced at the clock, seeing it was nearly two o'clock. "Oh, I almost forgot, Nan called a special meeting of the Frontier Days committee here at two."

"What do you suppose that is all about?" Betty asked, closing the notebook planner she'd created for Hank's and Julie's wedding.

Julie stepped from Hank's embrace and saved her work online. She grabbed Hank's hand. "Come on, this won't take long. Then I've decided to take the afternoon off and spend it with my favorite guy. Clay has got the boys helping him up at the house today." She glanced over her shoulder. "I have a feeling Sally has morning sickness."

Hank's brows rose. "Good lord. There are babies everywhere," he said.

"Which means we should probably get busy, huh?" she said, walking ahead through the kitchen.

He tugged her to a stop, and she turned to look at him. "What is it?" she asked.

"Do you mean that?" He took off his hat, holding her gaze.

"You mean, do I want more kids?" she asked. "I'd hoped you would want them, too. Don't you?" It was yet another topic they hadn't discussed.

He blinked and his face broke into a wide grin. "More than anything, I want to have kids with you."

She shrugged. "Well, sir, we'll have to make that a priority before you head off to smokejumper training camp next spring to retrain with Pete."

He pulled her into his arms, squeezing her tightly. "You are a remarkable woman. Not many women would agree to the life of a wildland firefighter pilot."

She looked up at him. "I can't promise I'll always be as sure of it as I am at this moment. But if it's what you love, then we'll make it work."

He hugged her again. "We won't have to move. Pete wants me to help with the initial training, and then we'll discuss where we'll go from there. Any decisions on moving, we'll make together as a family." He looked at her. "I'm thinking seasonal might be the way to go. Maybe pick up another job around here in the off season. I want to be closer to home," he said. "Closer to my family."

"I do like the sound of that," she said. "By the way, your parents called, and they'll be coming to the wedding."

"Any word from my sister?" he asked.

Julie nodded. "Caroline responded with an email, saying she'd be here for the ceremony but won't need a cabin. She has to get back to Chicago that night."

"Yeah, small towns and ranches aren't her thing," Hank said.

"Sally mentioned that Caroline and Rein had dated back in college?" Julie looked at him.

He nodded. "Hot and heavy for a while. We all thought they'd get married. I think Rein thought they were headed in that direction, as well, until she took off with a guy to travel Europe."

"Poor Rein," Julie said.

Hank shook his head. "Oh, no. He dodged a bullet with that one."

"Hank Richardson, that's not a very nice thing to say."

"Hey, she's my sister, I ought to know," he said. "It's going take someone with the patience of Job, and maybe someone who doesn't wear one of these." He held up the gorgeous Stetson. "Caroline has set the bar pretty high when it comes to guys. I just think she's too tightly wrapped. A day out fishing on the river or hiking in the woods would do her a world of good."

"I've only met her the one time," Julie said. "But she doesn't impress me as the outdoorsy type."

"Hey, you two," Betty said as she stuck her head around the diner entrance from the kitchen. "Nan's here, and she brought Hunter with her."

Aside from helping with the broken axle on the trailer to be used for the parade, Julie' curiosity was piqued, that her suspicions about Hunter and Nan might have been spot on. While else would she have brought him to this special meeting.

Betty turned the sign on the front door to "closed" at Nan's request.

Coach Reed and Betty had already managed to

push a couple of tables together. Jerry sat at one end, Hank and Julie across from Nan and Hunter. Coach Reed sat at the opposite end of the table.

"Anyone need coffee?" Betty asked as she waited for everyone to get settled.

A knock on the door drew everyone's attention. Betty let Dalton in. "Hey, I came in Wyatt's place." He glanced at Hunter. "Unless he asked you already."

"Sit down, Dalton," Nan ordered. She scanned their faces. "This won't take long. Just have some things to get out on the table and then we can be done with them. Don't want folks waggling their tongues any more than usual," she said.

Betty eased slowly into her chair and put her hand on Jerry's arm. "Nan, dear, what is it?"

Nan glanced at Julie. "Many of you know that I was married to my husband, Andrew, for some forty years. Happily, I might add." She paused. "But before we were married there was a period of time just after high school when we'd broken things off between us." She looked down at the table. "It was me who caused it. Didn't want to get married yet. I don't know, maybe it was fear, maybe just being young and wanting the freedom to chase my dreams." She smiled. "Hindsight is always twenty-twenty." She looked at Julie.

Julie reached over and slipped her hand in Hank's.

Nan shrugged. "As it turned out, Andy moved to Billings and got a job. Until recently, I wasn't aware that he'd dated my best friend, Gwen Neely, during that time."

Nan stood with a deep sigh and braced her hands

on the back of the chair, scanning their faces. It was clear that what she had to say was not easy, but she'd never been one to candy-coat the truth.

"The bottom line here is that Gwen ended up having a son. It was Andrew's. She immediately gave it up for adoption and never told him, as Andrew had gone off to war by that time. He didn't find out until many years later that he had a son. And only recently did I discover this, through a letter Andy left me. " She shrugged. "He said in the letter that, by the time he knew, it wouldn't have made any difference. He felt that we'd had the life we wanted—that we'd been happy, even though we had no children."

All eyes were glued on Nan. Hunter placed his hand on Nan's and smiled softly up at her. Julie made the connection in her mind just before Nan revealed the decades-old secret.

"Hunter, as it turns out, is Gwen's grandson." She looked around the table. "His daddy was Andy's and Gwen's son." She looked at Hunter. "And, so too, my step-grandson."

Hunter glanced at those around the table. "The lawyer I hired to look into it is sending for the official adoption records, but the place, the time of birth—my dad's birthday—were written down in the letter my grandmother sent to Nan's husband," he said, looking at her. "Who is my grandfather."

There was a stony silence in the wake of the news. It was Betty who spoke first. "I'm getting coffees all around." She stood, grabbed a tray, and arranged several mugs on it before lifting the coffee carafe and setting it all on the table.

Hunter cleared his throat and continued. "Nan

has invited me to stay on a while longer so I can get to know my grandmother better. With any luck, maybe one day she'll recognize me. I'm told I'm a dead ringer for my dad."

Nan nodded. "I see Andrew in your smile, as well," she said.

"And"—he took Nan's hand and led her to her chair—"I want to get to know my step-grandmother better. What I've seen so far I really admire."

Nan smiled and straightened her shoulders. "Well, there you have it." She looked at the quiet group. "Figured this committee is about as good a cross section of townsfolk there is, so I wanted to make sure you all have my back when the rumors start flying around here. Anyone have any questions?"

Dalton raised his finger with a thoughtful look. "I do," he said, then looked at Betty. "You have any pie to go with that coffee?"

Julie grinned and met Nan's content, if not relieved, smile from across the table. Yet another new beginning in End of the Line.

CHAPTER ELEVEN

Hank literally questioned his sanity.

"You know everyone would understand if you scratched," Justin Reed said, tightening the strap on the padded vest Hank had chosen to wear.

"Doc says it's been six weeks," Hank offered with a slight shrug. "I should be good to go."

The man shook his head, eyeing him sharply. "Okay. I'll put you in at the end. You can watch some of these guys first, and if you change your mind no one is going to think a thing of it—except that you made the right choice."

Hank thanked the man and walked with a bow-legged gait over to the where Rein, Wyatt, and Dalton leaned on the fence. They'd been helping out with the chutes. Aimee had chosen to go to the MacKenzie house for the day and help Liberty and with her and Rein's newborn daughter, whom they'd named Alana, after Rein's mother. Cody, far too excited about becoming an older brother had elected to stay home as well.

"Howdy, pardners," Hank called out.

All three turned to look at him as he sauntered carefully up to the fence. "It's not easy walking in these chaps," he said, hiking one dusty boot on the bottom fence rung.

Dalton chuckled, trying to cover it with a cough. "Yeah, we can see that…pardner."

Rein leaned forward in the lineup on the fence. "Are you certain you want to do this?" he asked Hank. "Need I remind you that your wedding is in a couple of weeks?"

"Damn fool's gonna kill himself," muttered Wyatt, standing next to Rein.

"I'm right here, Wyatt," Hank said. "I heard that." He took off his hat and brushed back his hair. He caught Wyatt watching him.

"Then maybe you should take the advice." Wyatt pointed a finger at him. "This is no joystick you're about to put between your legs."

"What does Julie think of all this?" Rein asked.

Hank scanned the small arena that Justin and Rein had built. The stands were full. It was a beautiful, crisp fall Saturday afternoon. The parade that morning on the town square had been packed. The junior roping contest and the exhibition barrel racing had been run and the amateur bronc riding was the last event until later that evening when the professional circuit riders provided bull-riding as an exciting conclusion to the day's events.

All-in-all, the weekend had been a grand success and the tiny community would benefit from everyone's hard work. Hank's absence from helping out with preparations had made him feel like he hadn't done his part. This was his way of providing that with the purse at the end of the competition going to a great cause.

"Now, settle down, boys," came a feminine

WORTH THE WAIT

voice from behind them.

Hank looked over his shoulder and saw Julie walking toward him dressed in slim denim jeans, a turquoise rodeo shirt, and black vest. She wore dusty cowboy boots over her jeans, rocking the whole "rodeo queen" look and capturing his heart.

"Maybe *you* can talk some sense into this guy," Dalton said.

She sidled up next to Hank, threading her arm through his. "Why should I? My man is fearless, boys. You know he landed an airplane—"

"In a lake," the three said in unison.

"We've heard the story a gazillion times," Wyatt said, tipping his hat back to look at Julie. "Not that it isn't admirable. Personally, I call it damn lucky—but this...this is different."

"I have full confidence that he's going to walk away with the prize today." Julie looked up at Hank and smiled.

"Meaning you," Hank said, holding his hat in place as he leaned down to capture her lips.

"Okay, okay." Dalton lifted his palms. "Don't expend too much energy there, son. You're going to need every bit you can muster."

Hank laughed. After another quick kiss, Julie sashayed away, giving him a sexy glance over her shoulder.

Michael Greyfeather offered a nod of his hat to Julie as they passed each other. He walked up to Hank. "Do you remember what I showed you?" he asked.

"Wait. You approve of this?" Wyatt asked, nudging his thumb toward Hank.

Michael shrugged. "Not nearly as bad as crashing a plane into a lake," he answered.

Wyatt rolled his eyes, pulled out his cell phone, and began thumbing through, searching for something.

"What are you looking up?" Dalton asked.

"The number for Billings's emergency room," Wyatt answered, not looking up.

Emilee Kinnison ran up to her dad, who stood next to Hank. "Dad," she said, tapping his shoulder.

Dalton looked down at his daughter, who Hank thought was much wiser than her years. Julie had told him about her vision, but he hadn't seen Emilee since the crash until now.

"What is it, Em?" he asked.

"Chris and Kyle asked if I could come sit with them. May I?"

"Sure." He looked into the stands. "If your mom says it's okay and you guys stay together, that is."

"Mom's helping in the pie stand. Grandma and Betty are there—"

"You mean Mrs. Miller?" Dalton raised a brow.

Emilee glanced away. "I'm sorry, yes, Mrs. Miller. Anyway, they're taking turns watching Sawyer."

"Okay, it's fine by me. But you guys leave before the end and get back over to the pie stand," Dalton said. "There's a lot of people here and a lot more coming in for the show tonight."

"Thanks, Dad. Um, do you have some money?" Emilee asked. "I wanted to get a peach snow cone."

"I heard Coach Reed's wife concocted the syrup

from real Georgia peaches," Hank said. When he turned to look at the young girl, his leather gloves slipped from where he'd had them tucked in his belt.

Emilee bent down to retrieve them. She held them up to Hank, hesitating as she eyed him. "It was you. You were the one...in the dark," she said. "I had a vision when I picked up the pocket-knife that you gave to Kyle."

Hank nodded. "I was, it's true. But I got though it by the grace of God and the love and prayers of my family and friends." He smiled then and leaned down toward the girl. "Those gloves giving you any good vibes?" he whispered.

She closed her eyes, gently stroking the soft leather. Opening her eyes, her gaze met his. "You should be very happy with how the night turns out," she said with an excited grin. Then she plucked the ten-dollar bill from Dalton's hand and raced off.

Dalton glanced at Hank, then looked at his brother. "Ten says he wins it."

"Oh, come on, that's not fair," Wyatt said. He paused. "Then again, it could just mean he's going to get lucky." Wyatt looked at Rein. "You in on this?"

Hank sighed. "Again. Right here," he reminded them.

"I'll put in twenty that he wins." Michael leafed through his wallet.

Soon every male within twenty yards of where they stood was placing bets on whether he'd survive the ride or not. It was a humbling experience. Then he had a wonderful idea. "Okay, guys, if I survive and win this, all the money collected goes to the Montana Smokejumpers Training Camp for new equipment. Deal?" he asked.

"And if you don't survive," Wyatt said with a smile, "we can use it to pay for your funeral expenses."

Hank slapped the broad chest of the man who'd become like a big brother to him over the years—the bossy big brother. "Prepare to pay up, big guy," he said with a grin.

Hank walked up to the gate with a confident swagger. Eight seconds on the back of a horse. How hard could that be?

"That was the longest damn eight seconds of my life." Hank winced as Julie continued to wrap the bandage around his bruised ribs. "On or off a horse."

Julie had divided her week between attending a bridal shower, confirming menu plans and flowers, and attending an impromptu bachelorette party at Dusty's, all while helping Hank recover from his stint on a horse called Devil's Thunder.

"You're lucky to have walked away with a few bruises," she said, smoothing the bandage over his muscled torso. "That horse had a mean temper." She looked up at him, her palms resting on his muscular chest. "I don't know which is worse—seeing you tossed around like a rag doll or thinking of you fighting a wildfire." She tucked the edge of the bandage in and secured it with a clip.

He kissed her forehead and pulled her close, resting his chin on the top of her head. "A few

WORTH THE WAIT

bruises are worth it. Pete is very grateful for the money. It's going to help them update the equipment at the camp."

Julie looked up at him. "Are you going to be able to walk without your cane?" He'd managed to hurt his hip when the horse finally bucked him off eight-point-seven-five seconds after the buzzer sounded.

Hank gave her a lopsided grin. "Easier than landing a plane in a lake." He searched her eyes. "But I have to tell you, I'd much rather close the blinds and spend the day in bed with you."

"I'm sure that the people we invited to the ceremony and the reception would understand," she said.

Aimee had offered to house Hank, and Clay had offered to take the boys, but today—this time—she wanted her family together. She'd risen, showered, and as they all sat down to the large breakfast she'd prepared, they'd held hands and asked a blessing on the day together.

Prayer had never before been a large part of Julie's life, but after all they'd been through, it had taught her to be more aware, to be thankful of her many blessings—even the obscure daily things. She was grateful for finding Hank, a man so giving and loving to her and to her boys. If she had one fear, it was that she didn't know how Louis would handle the news of her remarrying. She'd decided not to tell him until it was absolutely necessary.

"Fair enough. Honey, did you see where I put that bolero tie?" Hank asked, rifling through the top dresser drawer. "Clay gave it to me and I want to wear it."

Clay was Hank's best man. Chris and Kyle would serve as ushers for the handful of guests, which included Pete, Rosita, and the guys on his team. The ceremony would be held under the gazebo in the backyard of the Kinnison main house. After ushering, the boys would then walk their mom down the aisle.

Most everyone in End of the Line had been invited to the reception. After breakfast, she and Hank had snuck up to the barn to take a peek inside. Vintage lighted chandeliers hung from the rafters above. Twinkle lights and grapevine curled around the posts. Giant, bright yellow sunflowers and bronze and purple mums dotted the tables and flat surfaces. Hay bales with quilts covering them were used as seating off the swept-clear dance floor. Julie couldn't contain her emotions at all of the love that had been poured out to them by the people she'd come to know as family here in End of the Line.

It was perfect.

Her cell phone buzzed in her pocket, pulling her from her reverie. Seeing it was a California number but not one she recognized, she frowned. "Hello?" she answered cautiously, wishing she'd just let the call go.

"Hello, sweetheart. I was just wondering when you were going to bring the boys out to see their father."

Her blood grew cold at the pompous tone in his voice. "I can't discuss this right now. I need to talk with my lawyer and see what works best."

"Clearly," he said. "Oh, and I understand con-

WORTH THE WAIT

gratulations are in order?"

Her heart stilled. How could he have known? "I owe you no explanation," she said.

"Oh, of course not, sweetheart. I really do understand, given that we didn't part amiably. But it doesn't mean I carry any ill-will toward you whatsoever...or the man, what's his name, Hank? That guy you're marrying."

She met Hank's gaze. He walked over and gently took the phone from her. It was only then that she realized she was shaking.

"Listen you ass wipe," Hank said. "Don't call this number again. Our lawyer will be in touch with you about the boys visiting you out there."

"Oh, your lawyer apparently hasn't given you my bit of good news. I've been released early for good behavior. Though I haven't quite decided where I'll be living yet, since the firm had to let me go. But I'll be sure to let your lawyer know. You're a lucky man, Hank. Have a nice day."

Hank tossed the phone on the bed and drew Julie into his embrace.

"How could he have known?" She pressed close, wanting the shaking to stop.

"We'll change your number, first thing. I don't know, maybe one of the boys mentioned it when you called him about Chris." He stroked the nape of her neck where she'd twisted her hair into a soft chignon for the wedding. He held her at arm's length. "We're not going to let this ruin our day, Jules. He's a million miles away." He tipped up her chin to look at him. "And you know what would happen if he ever dared to show up here, right?"

Julie nodded. "I'll try. It's just that I hate having to take the boys to see him."

Hank held her gaze. "Only until they are fourteen. Then it'll be their decision. It was the only way we could get him to sign the divorce papers."

"I know," she said, pulling him close. "It's a chapter of my life I wish I could forget."

"It doesn't matter. You have primary custody of Chris and Kyle. And you have me." He looked at her. "Honey, there are a lot of things in my life I'd like to forget, but it's like our wedding song says, God blessed the broken road that led me straight to you."

Julie smiled, tears trickling down her cheeks. She searched his eyes and saw her future. "Hank Richardson, you are my hero, my best friend, my love. I never dreamed I'd find a man like you, but it was definitely worth the wait."

DEAR READER,
I hope you enjoyed following Hank's and Julie's journey to their happily ever after. (Hopefully, Louis won't give them any more trouble, but I'm not betting on that!) Theirs is a second-chance story to be sure, but it's more than that. It's also about not being afraid to believe you deserve a second chance. And it's about taking a step of faith, that things are going to be better than your previous broken experiences. I'm sure there will be new "potholes" on their journey, but with family, faith, and friends, they will face them together. As Betty often says, "Folks who are searching for a new beginning quite often come to End of the Line."

A sneak peek at more books to come in the END OF THE LINE series!

THEN~

HURRICANE SEASON
(End of the Line novella)

Dr. Gavin Beauregard lost the only love he'd ever known to Katrina. Now, more than a decade later, he's drawn by his past to Evermore plantation and the blistering desire of an ancient legend freed by the melding of a perfect storm.

Caroline Richardson plans to spend a girl's weekend with a friend, but fate, fueled by a passionate legend has other plans as she and a handsome stranger get caught in a whirlwind of desire!

NOW~

JUST WHAT THE DOCTOR ORDERED
(End of the Line novel)

Dr. Gavin Beauregard thought when he dove back into his work and dealing with his twin girl's lives that he'd forget about the mysterious woman he'd met on holiday, forget the steamy New Orleans affair and the night that rocked his world. But the more he tried to push the woman from his mind, the more relentless his desire became to find her, and the more driven his hope that she'd felt the connection between them as he had.

Caroline Richardson keeps her nose in her work. With barely time to date, she surrenders to the plea of a friend to join her for a girl's weekend in New Orleans. Fate steps in and she finds herself embroiled in a torrid one-night stand with a smart, handsome stranger that throws her ironclad plans into a tailspin. Though they agreed not to exchange names, forgetting it happened isn't working. And what Caroline wants, Caroline gets.

Excerpt from
Just What the Doctor Ordered

IT HAD BEEN AN EXQUISITELY small-town affair. Gavin scanned the lavishly decorated barn. The Kinnisons' Last Hope Ranch was spectacular, to be sure. One of the finest equine rescue operations in the state, but how they'd managed to turn the old barn into a wedding from the pages of Town and Country was beyond him. He'd seen many a reception in his day. Down home in New Orleans, he'd experienced the best of luxurious southern hospitality through the ties his father had as head surgeon and the social connections of his philanthropic mother. This, however gave new meaning to down-home hospitality. It wasn't that he was a snob. Not by any means. He'd traded out a cushy offer as head pediatric surgeon under his father's watchful eyes back home for a remote cabin outside of Billings, Montana. Finally, he was able to breathe from the stifling pressure of his father's constant scrutiny. He was on his own, building a clientele and enjoying the solitude—mostly. Though he was having a hard time dismissing the memories of a recent trip back home where he'd met a beautiful woman at a fundraising event for the National Pediatric Foundation.

His body tensed at the memories. What was to have been a tropical storm turned ominous and took out the power at the old plantation. Hunkered down, the entire reception of about fifty people, including the plantation owners and staff, waited out the storm in true Louisiana fashion—the champagne flowed and the food was plentiful. God, she was beautiful.

Gavin swirled the ice in his bourbon, swallowing hard against the image of her dark eyes, and sultry charm. Traditionally, he was not prone to one-night stands. But between the wine, the storm, and the seductive ambience of the old plantation home, he found himself in the arms of a stranger, doing things that even now caused his blood to heat.

He'd chosen a table in the corner shadows, observing the crowded dance floor, lost on his thoughts

"Hey, glad you could make it." Clay Saunders raised his beer bottle to Gavin as he walked over and pulled up a chair to sit next to him.

"Wouldn't have missed it for the world," Gavin said. "Looks like pretty much everyone in town is here."

Clay chuckled. "If there is one thing End of the Line folk know, it's how to throw a great party."

WORTH THE WAIT

"Hey, I haven't had a chance to ask. How's Aubrey doing?"

Clay grinned, his face expressing the immense pride and joy in his twin girls and their beautiful mother, who was currently out with both on the dance floor. "Starting to climb on everything. She and Ava are starting to get around. But Aubrey, she's my holy terror—a climber, that one. Ava is noisy—we almost always know where she is and what she's doing. Aubrey, on the other hand... she's fast and quiet. Who'd have thought given the rough start she had at birth that she'd have no fear?" Clay smiled in his thoughts. "The little dickens found a way to push open the screen from their second-story room and toss their toys to the ground. Sally had me install wrought-iron kick plates to the lower half of the windows so the little turd couldn't crawl out."

Gavin laughed out loud at the image. It never got boring, hearing what kids managed to achieve. It'd been one of the reasons he'd chosen the pediatric field. His gaze caught the bride and groom welcoming their guests to the reception. They were radiant. "Your sister looks lovely, by the way," he told Clay. "Sorry, I wasn't able to get to the ceremony. Had to run into work for a bit."

"That's okay, man. Glad you're here. Hope you can relax and enjoy tonight."

Gavin glanced again at the happy couple. Julie's new husband had spared no expense in the countrified party—from the chandeliers hanging from the rafter beams to the silk bows tied on every chair.

Gavin hand stopped midway to his mouth as a

woman entered, pulling in both bride and groom in a warm embrace.

"Dr. Beauregard," came Clay's voice from inside the hurricane wind swirling in his brain. "You okay, man?"

Gavin blinked, forcing the tongue from the roof of his mouth. What were the odds it could be the same woman he'd…well, let's just say they hadn't bothered with names—it'd been *her* choice, not his. "That woman who just came in. Do you know her?"

Clay glanced over his shoulder. "Sure, that's Hank's sister. She lives in Chicago. City girl through and through."

Gavin couldn't pull his gaze away, observing her animated conversation with the bride, the way her soft pink dress followed her every curve. Tonight, she had her hair swept up, tendrils teasing her neck. He remembered the soft, scent of her skin, the spicy, floral perfume she wore.

She paused then, and as though in slow motion turned her head and met his gaze across the room.

It was hurricane season all over again.

HERE IS WHERE IT ALL BEGAN...

THE KINNISON LEGACY TRILOGY

When tragedy strikes the lives of three young boys, they are placed under the care of wealthy cattle baron, Jed Kinnison. He raises the three as his own, leaving everything to them, including a special dream he had for the ranch.

Rugged Hearts
Rustler's Heart
Renegade Hearts
All I Want for Christmas

LAST HOPE RANCH
(series)

A string of cabins built next to the ranch built by Rein, Dalton, and Wyatt to fulfill Jed Kinnison's dream. Renamed Last Hope Ranch in Jed's memory, it is a sanctuary set in the beautiful ranch country of End of the Line, Montana to those in need of healing, and second chances.

No Strings Attached
Worth the Wait

END OF THE LINE
(small town series)

Heartfelt stories of the secondary characters, some familiar, others new visitors to End of the Line. As always served up with hefty slice of small-town drama, romance, and more in the once historic mining town. As Betty says," Folks who are looking for a new beginning find themselves at End of the Line."

Lost and Found
Georgia On My Mind
Hurricane Season

ABOUT THE AUTHOR

Published internationally in print, eBook, and Audio, bestselling author Amanda McIntyre finds inspiration from the American Heartland that she calls home. Best known for her Kinnison Legacy cowboys and Last Hope Ranch series, her passion is writing emotional, character-driven contemporary western and historical romance. Amanda truly believes that no matter what, love will always find a way.

CONNECT WITH ME HERE:

Website:
www.amandamcintyresbooks.com

Amazon Author Page:
http://bit.ly/AmandasAuthorPage

Book Bub:
http://bit.ly/AmandasBookbubPage

Goodreads:
http://bit.ly/AmandasGoodreadspage

BOOKS BY AMANDA MCINTYRE

CONTEMPORARY WESTERN ROMANCE:

KINNISON LEGACY:
Rugged Hearts, Book I
Wyatt & Aimee
Rustler's Heart, Book II
Rein & Liberty
Renegade Hearts, Book III
Dalton & Angelique
All I Want for Christmas
(Kinnison holiday novella)

LAST HOPE RANCH:
No Strings Attached, Book I
Worth the Wait, Book II

END OF THE LINE, MONTANA:
Lost and Found
Georgia on My Mind
Hurricane Season

CONTEMPORARY ROMANCE:
Thunderstruck
Stranger in Paradise
Tides of Autumn
Unfinished Dreams
Wish You Were Here

HISTORICAL:
A Warrior's Heart
The Promise
Closer to You (formerly Wild & Unruly)
Christmas Angel (formerly Fallen Angel)
TirNan 'Oge
The Dark Seduction of Miss Jane

HARLEQUIN SPICE/HISTORICAL:
The Master & the Muses *(audio/international)
The Diary of Cozette *(audio/international)
Tortured *(audio/international)
The Pleasure Garden *(audio/international)
Winter's Desire *(audio/international)
Dark Pleasures *(audio/international)

Made in the USA
Lexington, KY
21 December 2018